Only Son

This is a work of fiction. Any resemblance to actual persons, living or dead, business establishments, events, or locales is entirely coincidental.

ONLY SON – Pamela Meister/Shawn Goodwin
Published on March 17, 2012.

ISBN-13: 978-1470094911

Edited by Autumn Conley

Cover photo by Dennis Merrigan

Acknowledgments

This book, the first for both of us, could not have been completed without the help, guidance, and support of a few exceptional people. From me (Shawn), special thanks go to Detectives Dominic Pugliese and Robert Redanauer of the Philadelphia Police Department, true veterans who have taught me so much about the job I love. Thanks also go to Officer James Duffin, whose tactical knowledge proved invaluable during this endeavor.

Chapter One

His breath came out in short, painful gasps, causing the windshield to fog up. The interior of the car was stuffy, despite the coolness of the spring night air. Sweat beaded the killer's forehead; his hands felt clammy on the steering wheel.

The darkness was all enveloping, despite the lights that were still on in a few homes nearby. No one would be watching, for it was a neighborhood where people minded their own business and expected everyone else would do the same.

The killer could see the man in the road. Everything was in place, and it had to be done. There was no turning back. The engine roared in his ears, crowding out any potential sound of conscience attempting to tell him any different. His foot pressed down on the accelerator, and the tires squealed as the car shot forward, sealing the fates of more than one person that night.

What a crappy day.

Linda Petrilli drove up Allegheny Avenue, her eyes bleary with fatigue and anticipating sleeping in the next morning. As an assistant manager at Borders, she'd had her fill of rude and obnoxious people, and Linda was looking forward to what was left of her Friday night, devoid of the sights and sounds of other human beings.

Perhaps if she and Brian were still an item, she might have reconsidered her plans for the evening, but seeing as how she'd given him his walking papers three weeks earlier as a result of his cheating on her with that skanky Janet Fullman, it was yet "another Friday night, and I ain't got nobody" kind of night.

Of course, considering how many people had gotten on her nerves that day, that didn't bother Linda too much. Three of her workers had called in sick, which made for longer lines and shorter tempers at the checkout. Then there was the usual episode: A customer without a receipt demanding a cash refund for an item they may have never actually purchased in the first place. Borders had a very lenient return policy, and anything the store stocked could be returned for a store credit if the customer didn't have a receipt, but there was always someone who wasn't satisfied even with that. In this particular instance, the loud, large, overbearing woman had argued with Linda for nearly ten minutes before she finally left, store credit in hand, complaining loudly about the Borders return policy and the "goddamn managers," declaring that they "don't know anything." *Do people like that realize how much other people looked upon their behavior with disdain? Even if they do*, Linda thought, *they probably didn't care*. And this recounting of the day's aggravations didn't even take into account her morning, which had consisted of two exams and a presentation on which she depended for one-third of her course grade.

Linda could only thank God she'd be graduating soon. A student at Temple University's Fox School of Business, Linda would be getting her BBA in marketing in May. In just a couple of months she could look for a job in New York City and get the hell away from Philadelphia. No more Borders, no more crappy apartment on Jasper Street, no more having to avoid Brian's phone calls, the pathetic brute begging her to take him back.

Thursday nights were the worst. After going to class all morning, she had to work the late shift until 11:00, but she usually didn't get out the door until at least 11:30. Thank goodness she didn't have classes on Fridays. She'd wanted to go to school out of state. Even Drexel would have been preferable, but her parents just couldn't afford it. So with the help of a couple student loans and the job at Borders, she'd at least been able to share an apartment with a friend during her senior year and stop commuting from her parents' house in nearby Bensalem. Her 1999 blue Ford Escort was still in decent shape, but she was looking forward to being able to sell it if she managed to find a job in the city.

Linda yawned. It was coming up on 1:30, and she was totally wiped out. It didn't help matters that she'd had to stay later than usual to supervise the setting up of some sale tables. Turning onto Jasper Street, her tired eyes started scanning the side of the road for a parking space. As usual, parking was at a premium, and getting a spot right in front of her house was something that rarely happened. It seemed this night was not going to be any different. Resigning herself to having to walk a fair distance, she cruised slowly.

As she peered through the darkness, she saw something that made her blood boil – an improperly parked car that took up far more than its fair share of parking space. And it wasn't just hogging valuable space; it was also posing a danger to other drivers, as its rear end was jutting out into the street. Fortunately, there was an open spot just a few feet away. Linda parallel parked, then fumbled in the dark for a pen and the small notebook she always carried in her purse.

Exiting her car and grumbling about the inconsiderate nature of others, Linda trudged down the sidewalk, pen at the ready to jot down the license plate number of the offending car, but as she approached it, she stopped short, stumbling in her confusion.

The car, a dirty white sedan, was partially up on the curb. Just behind the front wheel on the passenger side was....*A body? Oh my God, it can't be!* But it was. Its legs were sticking out awkwardly, with the head and shoulders jammed in an almost unnatural contortion underneath. One foot had a running shoe on, but the other was shoeless. Linda stopped in her tracks and held her breath. After a moment or two, she realized there was no movement at all. Feeling bile rise in her throat and a pit of fear settle in her stomach, Linda dropped the pen and pad and found her cell phone at the bottom of her purse. With shaking fingers, she dialed 911.

Detective John Bell from the Homicide Division eased his car down Jasper Street. The bright lights of the police cruisers competed with the bright lights of the Kensington and Allegheny "El" Station, breaking up the gloom of a cloudy April night. A small group of nosy neighbors was being kept at bay by yellow police tape and a couple of uniformed officers at the scene. Ignoring the fire hydrant, Bell pulled into the only empty spot nearby. The call had roused him from another boring night on the graveyard shift, where he and his partner Nicole Ellis had been answering strange and inane phone calls from the locals.

The crime scene was located in the 24th District, deep inside East Division – a hotbed of every crime imaginable, from drug sales to homicides. The neighborhood is an old one, a fact that was immediately confirmed at the sight of some of the dilapidated row homes, but it is also a community with strong roots and for some, immense pride. While many of the citizens who grew up on these streets have moved to other locations, they always come back to visit "the neighborhood." Some of the older residents remember this section of the city as the neighborhood where the *Rocky* films were shot, and oddly enough, two of the film's main locales – Rocky's home and Adrian's residence – were situated inside the 24th District, just blocks away from the murder site; they look exactly the same today as they did three decades ago. The more things change, the more they stay the same.

Philadelphia is best described as a city of neighborhoods, and almost every section of the town carries its own name and its own unique charm. In Kensington, there is a burgeoning Latino population, but less than a mile away, a large Polish demographic makes up Port Richmond. Patrol officers in this division always laugh at the thought that they can find great *pinchos* at one diner and great *pierogi* at another diner three blocks away.

The two detectives made their way to the scene. Close on their heels were Detectives Brian Karpinsky and Bill King, who would be helping them with the initial interviewing and fact-gathering at the scene. Karpinsky knew the area well. His parents had immigrated to the States from Poland, and he'd grown up in nearby Port Richmond. Walking down Jasper Street, he thought it was a damned shame what had happened to the once proud neighborhood.

"What've we got?"

"5292, under the car." The uniform pointed toward the front of the white sedan. Back in the old days, the final four digits of the medical examiner's phone number were 5-2-9-2, and the odd label for a dead body had stuck.

"Who called it in?"

"Lady by the name of Linda Petrilli. She's sitting in the squad car over there."

Bell glanced over to see a woman huddled miserably in the back of a nearby police cruiser. He'd chat with her later; first, he wanted a closer look at the crime scene. He and Nicole both knelt down carefully so as not to contaminate the immediate area.

The car was an older model Chrysler Sebring. Underneath it, the body lay in a disheveled state. Nearby, on the street near the curb, was one running shoe, and the foot it had come off of was still wearing a somewhat dirty sock. Even in the dim light, they could see that there was little or no blood at the scene. *Was the victim run over?* They wouldn't know for sure until the body was pulled out and examined further.

Other than the stray shoe, nothing seemed out of place – if such a thing could be said about a crime scene. Looking closer, Bell and Nicole could also see that the victim was dressed in wrinkled khaki pants, and there was a noticeable bulge in the front right pocket.

"Maybe it's a wallet."

"Yeah, and if it is, it means robbery isn't likely the motive." Bell took his penlight out of his jacket pocket and flashed it under the car. Due to the angle, it was difficult to see much of anything. Returning to the uniformed officer he'd spoken to earlier, Bell questioned him further.

"Did you run the plates yet?"

"Yep. Stolen two weeks ago from one Sarah Jones of Lycoming Street."

Bell nodded to Nicole, who jotted the information in her notebook. "We'll talk to her tomorrow. What about the woman who found it? Petrilli, did you say?"

"Yep, Linda Petrilli. She was on her way home when she noticed the car parked at an awkward angle and was ready to report it to be towed. Guess she got a nasty shock when she saw what was underneath it."

"Okay. King, start knocking on doors. Someone has to have heard or seen something."

"Will do," said King. "Don't know how much we'll get though. This neighborhood isn't exactly known for cooperating with the police."

"Something's bound to come up." Bell motioned toward the small crowd of onlookers. "What about this group of jokers? Anyone see anything?"

"No...but then again, it would be hard to get anything out of them one way or the other. Most of them don't seem to speak much English."

As they spoke, the few onlookers began dispersing and heading back into their homes.

"Right. Karpinsky, see who you can snag before they take off."

Bell sighed, running his hand over his short, spiky brown hair. Like any major city, he knew Philadelphia was a hot spot for new immigrants. Historically, a large immigrant population in a city wasn't unusual, and that fact didn't bother Bell. What did bother him was the growing number of illegal immigrants flocking to Philadelphia and other cities around the country. (The city's official population hovers around 1.5 million, but the illegal population is thought to be anywhere from 10,000 to 20,000, mainly from countries like Brazil and Ecuador.) McPherson Square is a popular gathering place for day laborers as they wait for less-than-scrupulous contractors to pick them up for a day's work behind a shovel or putting up drywall. A few years back, Bell recalled that activists had gotten up in arms about some proposed federal legislation that would have made it more difficult for illegal aliens to enter the country and even harder to stay if they did manage to get in. There had been protest marches, angry letters to the editor of the local paper claiming "no human being is illegal," and other such softhearted claptrap from people whose lives weren't impacted by the influx of illegal immigrants.

Bell, however, was impacted. The increase in illegal immigration in recent years had coincided with an increase in crime, violent and otherwise. Rape, assault, fraud, drunk driving, and yes, murder were all on the rise. And because they were afraid of being reported and deported, illegals either didn't report the crimes or remained tight-lipped when questioned; thus, many of these incidents had gone unsolved and ended up in the cold case files. It didn't help that many of them either couldn't - or wouldn't - learn English.

Bell understood that city administrators had a thin line to walk. Citizens and other legal residents were getting fed up with the situation, but they didn't want to seem like cold-hearted bastards when it came time to head to the voting booth, so they did what politicians often do in sticky situations: They blathered on and on about how concerned they were about the number of illegal immigrants but passed the buck off to the Feds, claiming it was not the problem of the local law enforcement. In fact, the official line at the police department was that asking about someone's legal status during a routine crime investigation was *verboten*.

Officers like Bell knew the temptation for the people to illegally cross the border or overstay their visas; it was entirely understandable, all things considered, and there wasn't much to recommend their home countries. Governments known for corruption and a general disregard for the needs of the masses meant earning a decent wage to support one's family could be next to impossible. Taking a chance by crossing the desert or being packed into a tractor trailer (after paying a fortune to the smugglers, who were known as "coyotes") in order to get a job picking produce, working as an underpaid housekeeper, or digging ditches seemed like the right thing to do.

Nevertheless, no matter how dire their situation at home, Bell was under the impression that breaking the laws of America by entering the country illegally and without following proper protocol should have been grounds enough for deportation. Yes, he could sympathize, but he had sworn to uphold the law, and it galled him that he was ordered to look the other way regarding one of the most basic laws of the land. Unfortunately, he didn't see it being resolved anytime soon. He thought it was too bad more states hadn't taken the same stance as Arizona, which had passed a law giving law enforcement officers more authority when it came to detaining those whom they believed were in the country illegally, if they were under suspicion of committing another crime.

"Is the M.E. on his way?"

"Yes, sir. He should be here soon, along with the Crime Scene Unit."

"Okay. Make sure we get Police Tow here too. In the meantime, we'll talk to Miss Petrilli to see if she can give us any helpful information." Bell headed over to the squad car with Nicole in tow, digging her notebook and pen out of her shoulder bag.

Linda was still hunched in the back seat. A blanket had been draped around her shoulders, and she rocked gently back and forth in a way that put Bell in mind of a patient in a psych ward.

As she began to emerge, he waved his hand at her.

"Please stay where you are. There's no need to get up until you're ready to head home. Linda Petrilli?" She nodded, her dark blue eyes looming large in a face that seemed a few shades paler than its normal hue. Short, dark curls framed that pale face, and Bell could see that she was visibly upset. *Understandable.*

"Can you tell us exactly what happened?"

"I already told that other guy."

"I realize that, ma'am, but we're the investigating officers. I'm Detective Bell, and this is Detective Ellis. Just a few minutes more of your time and you can be on your way."

Nicole gave an encouraging smile. "We know it's difficult for you, but please, whatever you can tell us will be really helpful," she added.

"Well, I was driving home from work,"

"Where's home? Where's work?" Bell queried.

"I live just down the street, in an apartment with my friend Kim. I work part time at Borders as an assistant manager."

"Just part time?"

"Well, I'm also a business student at Temple. I'm supposed to graduate in May." She paused, picking at a lint ball on the blanket.

"Go on," said Bell.

Nicole wrote the information down. Her small, neat penmanship was much more readable than his prehistoric-looking scrawl, so the note-taking was generally left to her when they interviewed someone together. It was nice to be able to go back and read what was written.

"And, um, well, I was looking for a parking space on the street."

"Go on," said Bell.

"Okay. Well, I saw that white car sticking out into the street, and I got pissed off. I mean, not only could it have caused an accident, parking all crazy and hanging out in the road like that, but parking around here is a big enough pain without having to deal with idiots who can't parallel park. After I found a spot for my own car, I walked over to get the license plate number so I could report it." She paused. "That was when…when I saw…uh, when I saw - it."

"The body?"

"Yes." Linda sniffled, closed her eyes and ran the back of her right hand over them. "I've...I've never seen a dead body before."

Nicole stopped writing. "We understand, and it must have been quite a shock. Take a moment if you need to." Tendrils of her blonde hair, pulled back into a ponytail, were beginning to curl around her face in the humidity of the spring night.

"Well, that's really all. When I realized what it was, I called 911 from my cell phone."

Bell leaned against the passenger door. "Did you see anyone?"

"No."

"Hear anything unusual?"

Linda bit her lip. "No. Just the usual stuff - barking dogs, traffic on the main road, loud music from the house a couple of doors down from mine, you know."

"Did you recognize the victim?"

"How could I? I couldn't see anything but his...his legs sticking out. One of his shoes was missing."

"How do you know it's a 'him'?"

"I don't. I just assumed...I just said 'him,' okay?"

Nicole cast her partner a displeased look.

"Is there anything else you can remember that you might have seen or heard?" Bell urged.

Linda shook her head.

"Okay." He pulled a card out of his jacket. "We'll need a formal statement, but it's late, and I'm sure this has been upsetting for you. We'll be in touch about that, but in the meantime, if you think of anything else that might be helpful or if you have any questions for us, please contact me. You can go home now and get some rest." He and Nicole walked back toward the white sedan.

"She doesn't know anything. She was just in the wrong place at the wrong time," said Nicole.

"Probably, but you never know."

The area around the white sedan had become a hive of activity. Both the Police Tow and the Crime Scene Unit had arrived, as well as the patrol wagon that would be needed to transport the body to the morgue. Everyone on the crew was wearing their signature blue Dickies pants, blue golf shirts and jackets, and gloves so as not to contaminate the area. A photographer documented the scene, clicking away from every angle, while some took notes and combed the area for potential evidence, no matter how large or small. Still others were waiting to get their hands on both the car and the area underneath it, but the M.E. had to do his part first. Glancing around, Bell saw Dr. Gary Mitchell walking his way, his sandy hair tousled and yawning widely enough to split his head open.

"Ah, Dr. Mitchell, the man of the hour."

"Tell that to my wife. She hates these late night calls." Dr. Mitchell grinned boyishly as he opened his bag and, removed a pair of latex gloves, and snapped them on. "Anything you can tell me before I get started?"

"Not much. A young lady saw the body under the car and made the call. None of the neighbors seem to know much of anything, and the Crime Scene guys just got here. So really, the stage is set for your grand entrance."

Dr. Mitchell furrowed his brow as he jotted a few things down in his notebook. "When did she call?"

Bell caught Officer Blume's eye and waved him over. "Hey, when did the call come in?"

Blume consulted his notes. "Dispatcher took the call from Linda Petrilli at 1:43, and we got here at 1:48. Petrilli said she called as soon as she saw the victim."

Nodding his thanks, Dr. Mitchell knelt down to look at the body. "Weird position for someone to get run over."

Bell nodded in agreement, while Nicole observed, "Usually they bounce off the front end and flip over the car, ending up behind it."

"Yeah, that would make sense, but this looks more like the body was already lying in the street when the car ran it over - almost like it's supposed to look like a hit-and-run. Maybe he was a drunk who fell down in the street and got run over?" All the while they talked and speculated, Phil Lewis was dodging about, taking both color and black and white photos of the car, the body under it, and the surrounding area.

"Hey, Phil, how soon before we can move this hunk of junk and take a look?"

"Go ahead. I'm ready for the next step." As he instructed Officer Blume to get the tow truck going, Bell wondered how baby-faced Phil Lewis, the photographer, explained his job to friends and acquaintances. He imagined Phil at a bar, trying to pick up chicks: *"Oh, you're a photographer? Are you in the modeling industry?"... "No, I take photos of dead people." Oh well, it's not as though women are particularly impressed with my line of work either*, Bell thought. His ex-fiancée certainly hadn't been.

The tow truck had to back up onto the sidewalk because at that point, they just wanted to lift the front end of the car off the body; they weren't quite at the point where they wanted to tow it to the impound. As they waited, Bell could see various people peeking out of their windows, no doubt bothered by the lights and noise and wishing they'd all just go away. It was the same everywhere: No one wanted the cops around except when they were the ones in trouble.

Chains rattled, and the undercarriage of the Sebring groaned as it was hoisted into the air. When it was as high up as it was going to get, the driver gave them the all clear. Everyone looked down at the body lying in the street.

It was a black man with short hair. He looked to be in his early to mid-twenties. In addition to the wrinkled khakis, he was wearing a Philadelphia Eagles sweatshirt over a button-down shirt. They could see where the car had rolled over him. His eyes were open, wearing that cold, empty, glassy stare that indicated the occupant had vacated the premises permanently. There was very little blood, which was surprising, considering the nature of the man's death.

Bell and Nicole looked at one another, both thinking the same thing: *This will not sit well with the local chapter of Blaq Unity.* The activist group constantly harassed the police, claiming that black victims of crime received less attention than victims of other ethnic backgrounds. It was untrue, of course, as all murders were given the same priority level, except cases that went cold, forcing the diversion of manpower to newer cases. But facts don't always matter to groups with such a heavy axe to grind, and the two detectives knew they'd most likely be getting a phone call very soon.

After Phil took a number of photos, Dr. Mitchell knelt down to examine the body. After a few minutes, he looked up.

"Lividity and rigor mortis are starting to set in, so I'd say he's likely been dead for three to four hours. But take a look at this." Bell and Nicole joined him down on the ground as Dr. Mitchell used a pencil to lift up the back of the sweatshirt. "He's on his back, but the majority of blood pooling can be seen around the right side of his torso, and there's a large, paler area."

"So what does that mean, Doc?"

"It indicates that this man died while lying on his side."

Nicole and Bell saw the familiar purplish reddening of the skin with the startling pale patch. Lividity is a settling of blood in the body after the heart stops pumping, but the discoloration doesn't occur in the areas of the body that are in contact with the ground or some other object due to a compression of the capillaries.

"And there's more," Dr. Mitchell continued, gently probing the legs and ankles of the victim. "If this had been a hit-and-run, the legs and ankles would have multiple fractures from where the car hit our victim. From what I can tell, there are no fractures whatsoever."

Bell got up and walked slowly around the car. He stopped at the front, scratching his head. *No dent, no cracked windshield. If this guy was hit as he crossing the street, there not only would have been damage to the front end of the car, but the body likely would not have ended up under it. Hit-and-run victims usually bounce off and over the car, landing behind it. Hmm...* Bell remembered hearing about a horrendous case in Connecticut in which a driver hit a man crossing the street and kept going; the worst part was, no one stopped to help the victim for several minutes. It was all documented by a nearby security camera and made national news.

He called Nicole over, and they discussed his observations. The two detectives then looked at one another. "This whole scene has got to be a setup," Nicole said, brushing a tendril of hair out of her eyes.

"At first glance, yes," concurred Dr. Mitchell. "In any case, he didn't die here. Wherever he was killed, he was lying on his right side long enough for lividity to kick in."

"And evidently he was placed here, the car driven over him, and that was that," Bell said with a grim finality. "Nice."

"And before you ask, no, I don't know how he died. There are no visible wounds other than those inflicted by the vehicle, and if our theories are correct, we won't know much of anything else until the autopsy. This puppy's going to University City." All homicide and suspicious death autopsies in Philadelphia were conducted at the chief medical examiner's office on University Avenue.

"Ugh. Any idea when our guy will get a table?"

"Don't ask me. I'm just the prelim guy." Dr. Mitchell stood up, dusted off his gray slacks and tore off his gloves. "I'll write up my report and make sure you get a copy. I'm finished here. If you're going to do anything else, you'd better get it done before he's bagged and tagged."

The Crime Scene officers moved in like ants swarming over a dead grasshopper. They searched the area under the car for clues and, after more photographs were taken of the scene, instructed the tow truck to move the Sebring out of the way. "Hey," Bell said to one of them, "you see that bulge in his pants pocket? Could you get that out? We're thinking it might be his wallet, and if it is we might find out who it is." Moments later, the officer was holding a worn brown wallet in his gloved hands, and both Bell and Nicole crowded around it for a look. A driver's license could be seen through the plastic slot.

"Kevin Myers, address on South Street. At least he's one of ours," Bell said wryly.

"Anything else in there?" asked Nicole.

The technician rifled through the wallet. In addition to the license, it contained twenty-three dollars in fives and ones, a movie ticket stub, a debit card issued by Wachovia Bank, and a receipt from the Pathmark on Broad Street. Nicole snorted. "If it was a robbery, either they took the good stuff or killed him because he didn't have anything worth taking." She wrote the victim's name, address, and bank information in her notebook.

"So why didn't they take these?" Bell pointed to a couple of slips of paper marked "Dalia's Dollars," a form of currency used at a gentleman's club, an upscale strip joint called Dalia's Delights, located on Passyunk Avenue. Clients usually purchased Dalia's Dollars with credit cards, and the "money" was used to pay for things like private lap dances.

"I don't know. Maybe he didn't know what they were."

Bell laughed. Every warm-blooded male from Philly had heard of Dalia's Delights, even if he'd never had the fortune of visiting the establishment.

Nicole gave him a half-smile, conceding his unspoken point.

"That's assuming that a man was responsible for this. Anyway, he may have been forced to withdraw money from an ATM or two. We'll have to check with the bank about recent activity on his account."

Bell nodded, and the Crime Scene officer slipped the wallet into a plastic evidence bag and labeled it. They turned back to the body, which was being prepared for transport to the medical examiner's office. Paper bags had been placed over the decedent's hands and feet, and an identification tag had been attached to the ankle. A clean sheet was ready, and a body-bag on a gurney was being prepped. Dr. Mitchell was still hovering nearby, ready to seal and tag the bag once the corpse had been placed inside.

Nicole sighed and snapped her notebook shut. "So much for my weekend plans."

"Plans, huh?"

"Jeff and I were going to head up Route 263 and do some antiquing." Nicole enjoyed dragging her husband of two years to every single hole in the wall she could find that had an "Antiques" sign on the front door. They had just bought their first home in the Somerton area and, much to Bell's amusement and Jeff's annoyance, Nicole was determined to furnish it with as many "genteel" pieces of old furniture as she could get her hands on.

"Why the hell don't you just go to IKEA and get it over with?"

"Look, jerk, just because you've furnished your apartment in contemporary Neanderthal doesn't mean the rest of us want to live in similar squalor."

Bell laughed. "Hey, I like contemporary Neanderthal. It's become quite popular, ever since those insurance commercials with the cavemen." He ran a hand over his short, dark brown hair that had begun receding slightly and sighed. His plans for the weekend were far less eventful or romantic: sitting around and watching a bunch of action films he'd just received in the mail from Netflix, and those could wait.

Detectives Karpinsky and King approached.

"We've been up and down both sides of the street, and of course, no one's seen a damn thing. We also got a lot of 'no speak English.'"

"Crap. Oh well, there's always *mañana*. Besides, the media vultures will be swarming around, clamoring for information soon. Nothing like a good murder to get them all excited. The local rag will be thrilled, and their lousy circulation could use a boost."

"Come on," Nicole prompted. "You never know. The media could actually help us out on this one. Maybe someone will see the story and call us with some vital information."

"Yeah, right. And maybe some hack will end up getting an award for his crack reporting skills too." Reporters irritated Bell, and he didn't care who knew it.

The lack of any known eyewitnesses other than Linda Petrilli worried him as well. The first forty-eight hours after a homicide are the most crucial in an investigation. After that, with no solid evidence or clues, the likelihood of solving the crime plummets dramatically. Inside, he knew Nicole had a point. Sometimes seeing or hearing a news report about a violent crime does prompt people to come forward with useful information. Unfortunately, Bell knew it could also prompt cranks to call in with worthless tips – all of which had to be investigated, no matter how wild they sounded. Some of those BS tips came from lonely people who craved attention, who wanted to be a part of something exciting. Others came from nut jobs who either believed they were psychics and could help the police solve crimes like on television, or from true psychos who heard voices in their heads. It was Bell's experience that murder brought out the worst in people – and not just the ones wielding the axes or brandishing the guns or administering the poison or running over people in the street.

Chapter Two

Friday was damp and dreary, a common mood for Mother Nature during Pennsylvania Aprils. A fine mist settled over the landscape, further enhancing the day's dismal feel. Bell and Nicole made their way in an unmarked department sedan down South Street to the address listed on the victim's license and found themselves in front of a small diner: it became instantly apparent with an upward glance that the late Kevin Myers had lived in one of the apartments above it. A check into city records indicated that the building was owned by one Reginald Durkin, who just so happened to be the proprietor of the restaurant, appropriately named Durkin's. There was a small parking lot behind the building, and from all the empty spaces, they assumed they had arrived between the breakfast and lunch rushes.

Entering Durkin's, they approached a slouchy, older man with short, graying hair, standing behind the register, counting what must have been the morning's receipts. "Reginald Durkin?" Bell inquired.

"Yeah. Who wants to know?" His lip curled slightly, surprisingly revealing teeth that would have rivaled any Hollywood movie star's.

"Detectives John Bell and Nicole Ellis." They flashed their IDs. "Could we have a few moments?"

"Why not?" Durkin slammed the register drawer shut and led them to a sagging booth in the back, near the entrance to the kitchen. Sliding into the seat across from him, Bell began.

"We're here about one of your tenants, Kevin Myers."

"What's he done?"

"What makes you think he's done anything?"

"Well, it's not every day that the cops come by asking about people, you know? I guess I made the wrong assumption."

"It's not what he's done, but what's been done to him. His body was found last night on Jasper Street near K&A."

Durkin sat up, the expression on his face changing from surly indifference to concern. "Oh my God! What happened?"

"It looks like he was run over." Since an official cause of death had not been given by the medical examiner and the autopsy was slated for later that afternoon - they followed general protocol and wouldn't give out any more information than necessary. "We don't have a warrant, but would it be possible for us to take a look inside his apartment? Just a routine check."

"Of course, of course. Just give me a minute while I get someone to come out and watch the front." Durkin slid out of the booth and made his way into the kitchen. Bell and Nicole also made to rise, with Nicole checking her beige slacks and cream-colored sweater for any bits of food that might have stuck to them.

"Charming place," she muttered. "Remind me never to eat here."

A faint odor of grease and overcooked everything permeated the air. A couple young men, both clad in the typical ragged jeans and t-shirts preferred by the adolescent, sat in a booth on the other side of the restaurant, picking at the remains of scrambled eggs and toast and chortling over some private joke. Meanwhile, behind the counter, a waitress with strands of faded brown hair straggling from her bun was making fresh coffee and wiping down counters. Bell idly wondered why Durkin didn't just ask her to watch the front, but it wasn't his place to ask.

As Bell and Nicole continued to look around, Durkin exited the kitchen with a plump older woman in tow; she took her place behind the register. "Okay, let's go." He jingled a key ring, and they followed him out the front doors to another door just to the left. Inside was a steep set of stairs and at the top was a narrow hallway with two doors on each side. Durkin selected a key and unlocked the first door on the right. They hesitated momentarily to allow their eyes to adjust to the dim light before entering.

The small apartment, which faced the street, consisted of a main living area, a galley kitchen, and a small bedroom, with nondescript brown carpeting throughout. The first thing Bell noticed was that there were no bloodstains on the filthy carpet and no obvious signs of a struggle. Since Kevin Myers had likely been killed the previous evening, it was doubtful that the deed had been done in the man's residence. They stepped inside.

"Do me a favor and don't touch anything," Bell instructed Durkin, who looked alarmed but said nothing.

A dilapidated tan couch, a matching armchair, and a couple small tables were the main features of the living room. A small television sat in the corner, and a bag of tortilla chips and a container of salsa littered the low-standing, flimsy coffee table that sat directly in front of the couch. A quick look into the kitchen and at the contents of the refrigerator (a few bottles of beer and some milk) only added feasibility to the detectives' collective assumption that Myers was a typical bachelor.

While Nicole went toward the bedroom, looking carefully before entering, Bell turned to Durkin. "How long has he been your tenant?"

"Just over a year. Actually, he works...er, uh, worked for me too." Durkin stuffed his hands into the pockets of his tattered black slacks.

"Oh? In what capacity?" Bell asked, noticing Durkin's slip-up of referring to the dead man in the present tense, a typical reaction upon hearing of the death of a friend, loved one, or acquaintance. Acceptance would come later.

"Kind of an all-around guy. He busses tables, mops floors, helps keep the kitchen clean, and I give him a break on his rent for just keeping an eye on things at night...or, uh, I did."

Nicole had returned and was taking notes, as usual.

Durkin eyed her. "I thought you said he had an accident? What's with all the questions and record-keeping?"

She flashed a brilliant smile. "Nothing to worry about, Mr. Durkin. Just a routine inquiry. Taking notes is just part of the gig."

"Oh, okay."

"Is there anything else you can tell us about Mr. Myers?" Nicole continued. "Friends, family? Wife, girlfriend? Next of kin will have to be notified of his death, so if you know anything about that, it would help immensely."

"Far as I know, he didn't have a girlfriend, and he didn't have many friends that I know of either. Kind of quiet guy, and he didn't seem to get out much. The only guys he seems to pal around with work at the restaurant. When he applied for the job and the apartment, at first he didn't know who to list as an emergency contact. Said he was an only child, and that both his parents died in some kind of accident. Tragic, if ya ask me. Anyway, he eventually he put down the name of some aunt and uncle who live in Georgia." Durkin took a hand out of his pocket and scratched his head, causing a few flakes of dandruff to fall onto his dark sweater.

Ugh! Get yourself some Head and Shoulders, Nicole thought, reminding herself again never to eat anything the man prepared.

"We'll need that information," said Bell.

"Sure. I'll have to dig it out of my files in my office."

"We'll wait here."

Durkin looked slightly surprised at their insistence, but shrugged his shoulders. "Uh, okay. Be back in a few minutes," he replied and headed back downstairs. As soon as he'd left, both Bell and Nicole donned latex gloves that they pulled from their pockets.

"Find anything interesting in the bedroom?"

"Not much," Nicole replied as they entered. An unmade queen-sized bed took up the majority of the room. Next to it was a small night table, and a tall chest of drawers stood to the left of the bed. On top of the chest of drawers were a couple framed photos: one of a small child and two adults, presumably Myers and his parents; the other, a portrait of Myers in an official Army dress uniform, the kind of photo that is usually displayed proudly by mothers on their fireplace mantels. Bell picked it up gingerly, looking at the face of a dead man who must have once had many hopes and dreams.

"He was in the Army."

"Guess so."

"Anything else?"

"Nothing jumps out at me, but you never know what'll come up when we search the place more thoroughly." Nicole looked at the thick patina of dust on the furniture. "Not much of a housekeeper, that's for sure."

"How many single guys do you know who are?"

"Well, *your* place isn't so bad."

Bell laughed. "You can thank my mother for that." His mother had always been too busy with volunteer work and other out-of-home endeavors to do much cleaning or even cooking, so Bell had learned to take care of himself and their home at an early age.

They wandered through the rest of the apartment, which didn't take long. The kitchen was obviously not used for much more than heating frozen dinners or takeout leftovers, and the bathroom didn't hold any big surprises either. As they moved back to the living room, Durkin returned clutching a file folder.

"Got it," he said.

Bell held out his hand, and Durkin handed it over.

"Thanks. Well, I guess that'll be all for now. We'll let you know what the next step is. In the meantime, keep this place locked up. Nothing can be done about it until we notify his aunt and uncle. I'd be surprised if he had a Will, so it'll probably take some time to work out how to dispose of his, uh…belongings."

"What am I supposed to do about the rent I'll lose in the meantime?" Durkin groused.

"Sorry," Bell replied. "We'll do our best to hurry things along, but the legal system moves at its own pace. Thanks again for your time, Mr. Durkin. We'll be in touch."

He and Nicole shook Durkin's hand and made their way down to the car.

"Well, what do ya think?"

"He seems harmless enough," Nicole replied, "kind of a tightfisted old bastard, though, worrying about the rent when his poor ex-tenant's in the morgue."

"Well, did you see that diner? Not exactly swarming with customers. It's not really a big surprise that he'd be worried about missing out on income. Obviously Myers wasn't paying him a king's ransom, but I'm sure every little bit helps." He looked at his watch. "Come on. I have to head up to the O.M.E. and you have to talk to the owner of the stolen car, but let's think about lunch first."

Nicole looked at her watch. "Listen, I have a doctor's appointment."

"What? We just started a fresh homicide investigation. Reschedule."

"I can't," she said blandly.

Bell frowned. "Is it...serious?"

"No big deal. I just have to see my gynecologist, and those appointments are a bitch to get in the first place. You wouldn't think ladies would be lining up to get in the stirrups, but go figure. Anyway, I should be out of there by two, and then I can go check in with the car owner. Okay?"

"Say no more. Your inner workings are your business. I'll give you a buzz when I'm done at the OME."

"Aye-aye, Captain." Nicole gave him a mock salute.

As he drove up I-76 toward the O.M.E., Bell was fully wrapped up in his thoughts, aided by the *swish-swash* of the windshield wipers, which had somewhat of a lulling effect.

At this point in the case, they had very little to go on. One man was dead, underneath a stolen car and seemingly run over, but the report of the M.E. on the scene indicated that he had died elsewhere, meaning the murder scene was simply a set-up. He was just a young guy living alone, his nearest family an aunt and uncle in Georgia, and according to his landlord – who was also his boss – he had few friends other than a couple of guys he worked with.

The Army angle was intriguing, though, and the formal military photo of Kevin Myers in his uniform didn't seem all that old. *Why wasn't he still in the service? Was he dishonorably discharged? If he'd served his full stint working for Uncle Sam, surely he coulda found a better-paying than working as a general dogsbody at a seedy little diner. They have all those training programs and GI Bills for college, don't they?* Something about it just didn't seem right. With any luck, Bell hoped the aunt and uncle in Georgia could help clear up some of the questions.

As he got nearer to his destination, Bell thought about the autopsy ahead. He didn't enjoy attending them, but over the years he'd at least gotten to the point where he was able to turn off the instinctive part of his brain that told him to get as far away from the gruesome spectacle as he could. Sure, he could have just waited for the initial report, but he believed being on hand to hear the M.E.'s direct observations might give him a better perspective on how the victim had died. Plus, seeing the victim laid out on the autopsy table like that gave Bell more of a sense of urgency about solving the crime. Someone, somewhere, was responsible for that person losing his or her life – often in a brutal and ghastly manner – and Bell was committed to finding out who that was and why.

Nicole had been visibly relieved to have been assigned instead to visit Sarah Jones about the stolen Chrysler Sebring. She hadn't been to many autopsies, but during the last one – a victim who had been dead for several days before being discovered – made her nearly lose her lunch, something Bell was careful not to needle her about. He remembered his first autopsy all too vividly. The assault on his sense of smell, the whining sound of the saw cutting into the skull, and the sight of a young woman who had been raped and then beaten to death with what turned out to be a baseball bat would be forever engraved in his brain. In fact, Bell never forgot any of the victims whose murders he'd been assigned to solve, but he'd learned to compartmentalize them so he could turn off the horrors when he wasn't at work.

It was this ability to compartmentalize unpleasant realities and move on from them that might have had something to do with his failed relationship with Renee. When they had an argument about something – and more often than not, the topic centered on the demands of his job – instead of analyzing what had happened, he put it aside, always meaning to figure it out later. Unfortunately, that undefined later never seemed to come, seeing as though he was often deeply involved in one case or another, putting his personal life on hold. Of course, from everything he'd heard and read about the differences between men and women, his practice of putting quarrels aside and moving on was typical. This tendency proved useful to him in his job, but not with women. So the day Renee told him it was over, he'd been completely blindsided. That was six months ago.

Still, he was moving on. The first few weeks had been unbearable, but the sting was slowly diminishing after Renee's parting shot (something about loving his job more than he loved her) and life was beginning to return to normal. Moving on was his new mantra, and he was doing his best to do just that.

Bell got off the highway at the University City exit, and within a few minutes arrived at the office of the medical examiner (the O.M.E.). Housed in a large, ugly building that looked like it belonged in Nicolae Ceausescu's Romania, the O.M.E. had been created in 1953 by an act of city council. Before then, the office of the city coroner had functioned much in the way it had during colonial times. After 1953, a physician board-certified in forensic pathology was required to run the show. Bell parked and, after checking in with reception, made his way to the morgue, wrinkling his nose at the familiar but unpleasant smell of linoleum colliding with Lysol. The best time he'd ever had there was before he was promoted to detective. He and his former partner had brought a body, and the intake doctor was gorgeous. She'd since moved on to greener pastures.

Dr. Sam Barnes and the corpse were waiting. "Right on time," Barnes noted, snapping on a pair of gloves. "Ready?"

"Ready as I'll ever be." Bell waved away the proffered mask. Tom, the assistant (called a "diener") rolled the gurney over and shifted the body to the two-tiered autopsy table. Then he unzipped the bag, which was searched for any potential trace evidence that might have shaken loose. He and Dr. Barnes then lifted the decedent's stiff legs and inched the bag down, bit by bit, until it was off. They unwrapped the sheet and examined it for evidence as well, removing a few fiber samples and placing them into envelopes. Every time any evidence, clothing, or jewelry was removed, the time was carefully noted and recorded.

Once the body's estimated height was recorded and the weight determined by the gurney being wheeled onto a large scale (with the weight of the gurney being subtracted), photographs were snapped from every angle. Barnes, dictating occasional notes into his handheld recorder, noted the lividity and lack of leg and ankle fractures that Dr. Mitchell had pointed out at the scene and the fact that the injuries to Kevin Myers's body by the car were post mortem. He lingered near the neck, scrutinizing it carefully.

"See this?"

Bell moved a little closer and peered at the victim's neck. He noted the horizontal mark on the skin, which had been partially hidden by the victim's sweatshirt – not near the jaw line, but further down. The mark was accompanied by bruising. He frowned.

"And do you see this?" Dr. Barnes pointed to the minute red splotches under the victim's eyes; they resembled tiny pinpricks.

"Petechial hemorrhaging."

"A-ha." Bell nodded. Petechial hemorrhaging is a sign of asphyxiation, caused when increased pressure to the veins in the head cause them to rupture, and blood leaks from the tiny capillaries in the eyes and face. The fact that they only appeared under the eyelids indicated strangulation rather than suffocation.

"We'll check for a few more things, like bruising of the larynx and hemorrhaging, but in my best estimate so far, I'd say it looks like a case of ligature strangulation."

"Any idea what was used? Rope? Wire?"

"It's shallow and broad rather than deep and narrow, so that probably rules out a wire or cord, but I'll have to get back to you on that."

Bell watched as Dr. Barnes and Tom continued to search for hairs and fibers on the body. When they had finished, they removed the paper bags from the hands and feet, taking fingernail scrapings and fingerprints, then began removing the clothing and putting it into separate evidence bags. More photos were taken to document everything.

A short while later, Dr. Barnes was ready to look inside. "Let's have a look at those lungs." Placing a hard rubber block under the head, he made the customary Y-shaped incision, then peeled back the skin, muscle, and soft tissue. After pulling the chest flap over the face to expose the ribcage, he made two cuts along each side of the ribcage and pulled it from the body, exposing the inner organs. He examined and removed the heart. Just as Barnes had predicted, the tiny red splotches were evident on the lungs.

Several hours later, the only other abnormal observation that had been made was a bruise on the back of the head, indicating that Kevin had either fallen or had been hit. Either way, it happened before his death. Stomach contents included what looked like tortilla chips and salsa, so the snacks Bell and Nicole had seen in his room were his last supper, of sorts, eaten only a couple of hours before his death. Other than his unnatural cause of death, he had been in general good health, and Dr. Barnes promised to have the full autopsy report on Bell's desk within a few days.

Nicole had been waiting in the examination room for what seemed like hours. Rather than sit on the high, paper-covered table with stirrups or the cheap orange plastic chair, she paced the small confines of the room, glancing at glossy brochures about the importance of breast self-examination and how to avoid sexually transmitted diseases. Normally, Nicole was a patient person, which fit in nicely with her occupation. She realized that doctors are busy, too, but today of all days, she was anxious and wanted to be anywhere but there.

She had moved from the brochures to a tattered copy of *Good Housekeeping*, six months out of date, when a sudden tap on the door preceded the doctor's entrance, causing her to jump and drop the magazine. The door opened as she bent down to pick it up.

"Mrs. Ellis, hello."

"Hello Dr. Grant." She fumbled to put the outdated issue back in the magazine rack on the wall. Dr. Grant was a pleasant-looking man in his early fifties, with a shock of white hair that made him look distinguished. He sat down at the little desk and indicated that she take a seat in the orange plastic chair she'd been avoiding.

She sat down carefully.

"Well?"

"Well," he said with a smile. "The test came back positive."

"Positive?" she said weakly.

"Yes, positive. Based on the information you gave me at your last visit, I'd say you are about six weeks along. Congratulations."

She smiled shakily. "Thanks."

After a few more minutes of conversation about what she could expect while she was expecting and when he'd need to see her next, Dr. Grant excused himself.

Nicole made her way out to the receptionist's desk to make her next appointment.

A few minutes later she was in her car with the keys in the ignition, but she just sat there. *Pregnant? How is that possible?* She and Jeff had always used protection. Of course it was never 100 percent foolproof, but for it to fail now was a huge deal. *Me, a mother? Yes, I want kids, but now? I'm not ready yet!*

Nicole was nothing if not meticulous about every aspect of her life. Nothing went unplanned. She was even known for choosing her wardrobe for the following day just before retiring to bed. Bell sometimes teased her about what he called her fussy, granny-like ways, but he also appreciated her thoroughness when it came to investigations. *God, Bell. What on Earth will he say about this? Hell, forget Bell, what's Jeff gonna say?*

23

She knew her mother would, of course, be thrilled. She was always dropping little hints, implying that if Nicole waited too long, she might be too old to conceive without expensive fertility treatments that would drain her financially and emotionally. The only fly in the ointment for her mother would be that Nicole's father wouldn't be there to share in the family joy.

Nicole rubbed the bridge of her nose, something she often did when conflicted. Yes, she and Jeff wanted a family, but not yet. They were both ambitious career-wise, and frankly, Nicole's job as a detective wasn't conducive to dealing with a baby. She'd fought hard to get where she was and knew that taking maternity leave now would set her back on the promotion track.

Of course, there was always the option of abortion, but she dismissed that thought almost as soon as it entered her mind. Nicole didn't believe that it was only a clump of cells inside her; in her opinion, it was already a life, and there was no way she would consent to having it sucked out of her in a cold, sterile room, something she and Jeff had created together, discarded in a clinic trashcan.

Turning the keys in the ignition, Nicole sighed. She'd figure everything out. She just needed a little time. For the time being, she had a job to do.

As he drove back to the Homicide Division, Bell mulled over what was known so far. Kevin Myers had been asphyxiated – possibly being knocked down first – and then his body had been planted under a stolen car to make it look like an accident. It might have taken place in his home, seeing as the contents of his stomach matched food left lying out there, but there was no sign of forced entry. Still, the apartment would have to be given a full onceover. According to his boss and landlord, Myers had no nearby family, no real friends besides a few co-workers, and he led a relatively quiet life. *So who would want him dead?* Then there was the Army angle. They'd have to check into his record. *How long had he been in the military? Why did he leave?* And while he didn't even want to consider the possibility, the killing may have had racist overtones. As Bell was navigating the rush-hour traffic, pondering all of this, his cell phone rang; Nicole had just returned to the police station. "Hey there," he said, "what did you find out?"

"Not much."

Bell adjusted his headset so he could hear better. "I spoke to Sarah Jones, and all she could tell me was that she parked her car on the street in front of her house a couple of weeks ago and when she came out the next morning to go to work, it was gone. At first she was excited that we'd found it, but she got pretty ticked off when I told her it was impounded and it'd be some time before she could get it back. I also contacted the local police down where the victim's aunt and uncle live. They're on their way to break the news, and then I'll call them. How about you?"

Bell related the results of the autopsy.

"So maybe our guy was killed in his own home and placed in a phony accident scene," Nicole speculated.

"I'm not sure about being killed in his own home, but it's a possibility we'll have to keep in mind. The CSU will have to give it a full going over. Listen, we're going to need to talk to his co-workers. I also want to look into the guy's military service. Maybe he pissed someone off when he was off soldiering."

"Strangulation doesn't seem much like a revenge killing. It's violent, sure, but it's over in just a few minutes and isn't…well, it isn't very messy."

"Maybe not, but we don't have much else to go on right now. Look, by the time I get back, it'll be close to dinnertime. Why don't we have a bite to eat at Durkin's?"

"What, with dandruff flakes and grease and all? Mmm, sounds appetizing…Not!"

"It'll be a chance to talk to Durkin again, as well as some of his other employees. Besides, you're always complaining about how difficult it is to keep your weight down. You won't have much difficulty sticking to your diet in that place." Bell chuckled at Nicole's feigned burst of outrage. "I'll meet you back at Homicide in about half an hour, and then we can head out. Listen, we're going to have to get a CSU team into that apartment ASAP. If that was, in fact, the initial crime scene, I hope we didn't mess things up too much."

"I'm on it. See you soon."

"Hey, wait a minute. How did your doctor's appointment go?"

"Fine," she said shortly. "Just a routine visit. See when you get back." She hung up.

Bell was surprised by the curtness in her voice and the abrupt way in which she ended the call, but remembering the nature of her doctor's visit, he marked it down to PMS or some other feminine situation he didn't know about. Renee certainly had been a bitch on wheels just before she had her period, so he could only assume it ran in the gender. He turned on the radio and sang – or rather shouted – to AC/DC's "Back in Black."

Back at the station, Nicole took her ash-blonde hair out of its pony tail and rubbed her temples, then slid the folder with Kevin Myers's rental agreement and employment application out of her bag. That was always the worst part – telling the family that a loved one had died – and murder made it that much worse.

She would never forget the day the police had come to her door with the news that her father had been killed in an automobile accident. Her mother had been cooking dinner when the doorbell rang, so little Nicole had run to answer it. She remembered the smell of the meatloaf in the oven as her mother collapsed into tears. Nicole had never eaten meatloaf since.

But while her father's untimely death was a blow that would always haunt her, Nicole had somehow escaped falling into the despair that others in a similar situation might have succumbed to. A loving and supportive extended family helped to ease the pain, as did Nicole's naturally sunny disposition. Only twelve years old at the time, she became her mother's right hand, helping to raise her younger brother and sister, yet still managing to keep her grades up and participate in extracurricular activities. The police officers who had come to the front door on that fateful day had made a great impression on her, and it was at that point that she'd decided she wanted to join the police department. Recalling the day she graduated from the academy, she could still hear the catch in her mother's voice as she told her, "Your father would have been very proud."

Now, with the news of the day, she couldn't help thinking about the painful reality that his first grandchild would never know him except from photos and stories. A twinge of sadness pricked her.

Nicole's aptitude for empathy was extremely helpful in her work. Whether she was dealing with murder or simply a stolen car, the victims always felt as though she really knew what they were going through. Pairing up with Bell had been a stroke of luck. His skill for problem-solving, combined with her habit of goal-setting and her ease in dealing with the public made them a very effective team. The only glitch in their professional relationship was Bell's occasional anger issues.

Nicole sighed, her thoughts turning from her own problems to her partner's. She wished Bell could find the same satisfaction in his personal life that she had enjoyed with Jeff since their marriage a couple of years before. When Renee broke up with Bell, Nicole had been disappointed but not surprised.

Renee was a rather needy individual, and Bell's independence combined with his unpredictable work schedule hadn't been quite what Renee was looking for. Finally, after a period of several months, she could see that Bell was starting to come out of his funk, and Nicole and Jeff were planning a picnic for Memorial Day, which would give her a chance to introduce Bell to a few of her single friends.

But that would have to wait. The phone rang; it was the cops in Georgia, telling her the deed was done. She hung up, then picked up the receiver again to dial the telephone number of Kevin Myers's aunt and uncle, mentally rehearsing what she would say when they answered.

Chapter Three

The Homicide Unit was located inside Philadelphia Police Headquarters on 8th and Race Streets, otherwise known as "The Roundhouse." The nickname was self-explanatory, as the building was an architectural travesty consisting of two circular three-story portions connected by a short, straight portion. Seen from above, the Roundhouse resembled a barbell. Some even joked that it looked like the Museum-go-Round from the *"Mister Rogers's Neighborhood"* children's television show.

As grotesque a structure as it was from the outside, however, the Roundhouse was considerably worse on the inside. Dank, dirty, and mouse-infested, Police Headquarters was a disgusting place to work. The stained, gaudy yellow linoleum floors clashed with the depressing faux wood paneling to render a montage of offensive sights and smells. Ironically, the prisoner holding cells received more attention from the janitorial staff than did the other offices, and city union contracts meant homicide detectives couldn't even change a light bulb on their own since that important task was reserved for a union member from Public Property. Of course, by the time someone from Public Property actually showed up, three or four more fluorescent bulbs had gone the way of the dodo, and the vicious circle of life continued onward.

The squad room at Homicide was no better. Despite what most people thought, Philly detectives did not work in spacious rooms with plenty of windows and Pergo flooring. In fact, Homicide was adorned with the latest in 1974 furnishings. Heavy steel desks that couldn't be moved with less than three men, file cabinets left over from the Eisenhower administration, and computers that were direct descendants of ENIAC were the norm rather than the exception. In fairness, the city was trying to shorten the great technological divide, but fiscal matters always outweighed employee comfort. As a result, many detectives purchased their own tools of the trade. Digital cameras, laptops, and zip drives were often part of a detective's personal stash, and they were always aptly and permanently labeled to prevent them from being "borrowed" without permission.

Bell always thought the Homicide Division deserved better digs, but he resigned himself to the fact that a new, clean building would never be part of the deal. *Besides,* he thought, *if it's good enough to house the police commissioner's office, it's good enough for me.* Still, he and so many other cops he knew couldn't help being ticked off while watching *"Cold Case"* because the sets were gorgeous and completely untrue to life. Bell and his co-workers could relate a lot better to the 1970s *"Barney Miller,"* with all its grit and grime.

Homicide personnel did not have "desks," per se, because there were not enough in the squad room for every detective. Thus, they would find an empty spot when they reported on for their shift and make it their home for eight-plus hours. Personal items were usually kept in drawers inside their file cabinets, and most detectives had something or other to give their workspace more personality. For Bell, it was his *Simpsons* daily desk calendar. Nicole always teased him about it – specifically, she joked that it was "juvenile" – but after sloshing through a day of dead bodies and grieving families, he needed all the laughs Bart and Homer had to offer.

Bell walked into the Homicide Division squad room feeling like a bus had hit him. Running on a homicide was tiring work, and it was even more difficult when officers had to spend eight or more hours in court. Bell always mused that Homicide is for the younger crowd, but he had to admit that younger detectives don't have the experience or the temperament most of the time, at least not without going completely and utterly insane.

For the time being, Bell could handle the insanity. Nicole always considered him a "302" anyway, the term for a mental health commitment. What he could not handle was the exhaustion. His mood was suffering for it, and it was about to get worse: His platoon sergeant was approaching, and that was always a cause for dread.

"Bell," the sergeant began, "what's going on with the Myers job?"

Itching for an argument, Bell sardonically replied, "He's still dead, Sarge."

Sergeant James Baker personified everything that was wrong with the Philadelphia Police Department. A hulking, heavyset black man, Baker had spent most of his twenty-year career studying for the next promotional exam instead of learning the job. After taking (and failing) the lieutenant's test for the fourth time, Baker used his considerable influence to land a transfer to Homicide. Sadly, that was how many of the division's subpar personnel arrived. Make no mistake: Philly Homicide was one of the best in the business, but every unit had its bad apples. Baker was the worst. To his subordinates, he was a martinet who was smart enough to know that he was the boss, but he was dumb enough (or cocky enough) that he never recognized when he was dead wrong – and that happened often.

Bell thought the man went out of his way to break his stones, but as Nicole always pointed out, Baker was an ignorant creep to everyone under his command and was an equal opportunity jerk. Nevertheless, the dance continued.

"Is that what you want me to tell the captain, Bell?"

"No, sir," Bell replied. "We're running on a couple of leads, and Nicole and I are still trying to sort out the interviews. The M.E. promised the completed autopsy report by the end of the week, so we should know more in a day or two."

Bell had a personal policy of only giving the sergeant enough information to keep him off his back. Anything else, and Baker – a man who couldn't solve a *Wheel of Fortune* puzzle without every letter exposed – would want to get involved in the investigation.

"Are you aware that Blaq Unity called the captain first thing this morning?"

Christ, thought Bell, *they must listen to police scanners*. The story hadn't even broken in the media yet. "No, sir, but rest assured this case is a top priority for us."

"Fine. Let me know the second something breaks," barked Baker before turning and walking away.

"Yeah, you'll be the first person I call…Idiot," Bell muttered. He wandered to his desk to wait for Nicole, who was on the phone.

The phone rang several times before being picked up by a woman. "Hello?"

Nicole ran her free hand along her slacks, her palm all sweaty. "Mrs. Myers? Mrs. Leon Myers?"

"Yes. Who is this?" Nicole could tell she had been crying.

"My name is Detective Nicole Ellis, with the Philadelphia police. I'm calling about your nephew, Kevin. I believe the local police were just there to tell you what happened."

"Yes." Mrs. Myers continued sobbing softly, and then Nicole heard a rustling sound as the phone was passed from one person to another.

A man spoke to her in a curt, clipped tone.

"Who is this?"

Nicole repeated what she had told his wife. "I hate to tell you this, sir, but we have reason to believe there was foul play involved in your nephew's death."

"Foul play? What does that mean?"

"It looks as though your nephew has been murdered, Mr. Myers. I'd rather give you the details in person. We need a close relative to formally identify and claim the body. I realize you're down in Georgia, but unless there's someone else I can call, you're it. I'm so sorry. Please accept my condolences." Nicole had to work to keep her voice steady. She knew firsthand how difficult it could be to accept the death of a loved one, especially when it was violent and unexpected.

The voice on the other end was not quite as belligerent as before. In fact, it sounded somewhat pleading. "Are you sure it was my brother's boy? Could there be some mistake?"

"That's always possible," Nicole conceded, "but we don't think so. He had photo ID on him when he was found. When we went to his apartment, we met his landlord, who is also his boss. He was the one who told us that Kevin had no immediate family in the area. Apparently, Kevin put you down as the sole emergency contacts on his lease. How soon will you be able to come up?"

"Hold on." Muffled conversation ensued, and then Leon Myers returned to the phone. "We should be there by Monday afternoon. I hope you're working on finding the bastard who did this." His voice was shaking.

"Believe me, sir, we're doing all we can. We want to find the culprits as much as you do."

As she hung up the phone, Bell looked at her sympathetically. "How'd it go?"

"As well as you might expect." She sighed. "They're coming, but I'm sure they're hoping that by the time they get here, we'll know we made a mistake." Nicole's own mother had been sure that the police had gotten it wrong when they first came to their home to inform them of her father's fatal accident, but that was not the case then either. "Anyway, I had another call before you got here."

"Oh?"

"Jean Gardner from *The Inquirer*."

"Damn."

"Don't tell me you thought she wouldn't find out about this. She's like a vulture."

"Of course I knew she'd be sticking her nose in, but hell, I'd hoped we'd get at least another day in before she came snooping around. You know, the newspaper industry can't collapse fast enough for me. When *The New York Times* goes, the others will follow. It will be a good day for the world." Bell scowled. As far as Bell was concerned, reporters were the bane of a police officer's existence: constantly nosing around, never minding whom they might hurt in their pursuit of a hot scoop that would earn them a Pulitzer Prize – or at least a bonus and the admiration of what peers remained in the ever-shrinking newsrooms. Bell knew the newspaper industry was experiencing hard times. This was due to a number of factors, including the information boom of the Internet, but because of his antipathy toward reporters in general, he felt little sympathy. He couldn't wait for the inky bastards to crumble. "What did you tell her?"

"As little as possible." Nicole laughed. "What do you take me for?"

Bell and Nicole entered Durkin's that evening. While the restaurant had customers, business wasn't exactly booming. Reginald Durkin was at his place at the register, and he seemed surprised to see them again. "Could we have a table?" Bell asked.

"Uh, of course." He showed them to a booth – the same booth they'd sat in before – and handed them a couple of dingy menus.

"Do you have time to talk to us in a little bit?"

"About Kevin?"

"Yes."

"Sure. Give me a minute." He slouched and shuffled back to the register to ring up an elderly gentleman's bill.

The two detectives sat in silence as they perused the culinary offerings. Nicole put her menu down first. She wasn't terribly hungry, and the morning sickness – which had been one of the first signs of her pregnancy – wasn't necessarily relegated to the mornings. The idea of eating anything heavy and greasy was too much, and that seemed to be Durkin's specialty.

"I'll just have a soup and salad. It can't be that bad," she said, hoping she could keep it down.

"Hmm. I'll go for the cheeseburger deluxe."

"How can you eat that crap and still stay thin? All I have to do is look at a cookie and I put five pounds on."

"Women..." he said, sighing and rolling his eyes.

"So, you were going to tell me about your conversation with Sarge?"

"Not much to tell. He wanted to know where we are in the investigation, and I told him we don't have a lot to go on just yet."

"And I'm sure you told him in the nicest way."

"Well, you know me. Mr. Polite."

"I'm telling you, John, it's not a good idea to get on his bad side." She gave him the sternest look possible for someone of her general good nature to dredge up.

Bell laughed.

"Look, Baker's hide is as thick as a rhino's. Insults just bounce right off. Don't worry about it. I know how far I can go with him."

Nicole was opening her mouth to retort when their waitress showed up with two glasses of tepid water. "Are you ready to order?"

After they placed their orders, Bell flashed his ID.

"I'm Detective Bell, and this is Detective Ellis. Would you have time to answer a few questions about Kevin Myers?"

The waitress pushed back a lock of crinkly brown hair that was escaping from its high ponytail. "Oh, yeah, I heard about the accident. It's too bad. Kev was a nice guy." She glanced sideways at Durkin, who was watching the exchange. "What is it you wanna know?"

"I'd rather wait until you have a few minutes." He flashed his most disarming smile, and the woman blushed faintly.

"Well, I got a break in about twenty minutes."

"That's fine. Can you join us here?"

"Yeah, sure."

As she walked away, Durkin returned.

"Everything okay?"

"Of course. Have a seat."

Durkin sat next to Bell, across from Nicole. While she was secretly relieved that he hadn't sat next to her, she wasn't sure having him across from her, in full view, was much better. She reached into her bag for her notebook and pencil, then held the notebook in front of her as she sat poised to take notes.

"So what's this all about? Did you have trouble getting in touch with Kevin's relatives?" Durkin folded his work-worn hands on the table in front of him.

"No. The information you provided was very helpful. Detective Ellis reached them this afternoon, and they'll be flying up from Georgia on Monday."

"I suppose they'll want to take Kevin's things home. Should I have them packed up?"

"Well, that's part of what we need to talk about." Bell leaned in a little closer to Durkin. "According to the autopsy results, Kevin didn't die in a freak accident. The accident was a hoax. It was staged."

Durkin's brow furrowed. "Staged? I'm not sure what you mean."

"Kevin was asphyxiated."

"Ass-what?"

"Asphyxiated, strangled, at least several hours before he was found on Jasper Street. Someone dumped him out on the street and ran a stolen car over him to make it look like an accident."

"You mean-"

"Yes, Mr. Durkin. Kevin was murdered."

Durkin wiped his hand over his eyes, and his voice sounded somewhat shaky. "I...God, I can't believe that. Who would want to kill Kevin? He was such a nice guy. Everyone here liked him, and he was a great worker. That's...it's such a shock." He sighed heavily. "So what's next?"

"We'll need to speak to everyone who works here, especially those who knew Kevin best, and we'll need to talk with any of your regular customers who came in contact with him."

"Of course, of course. Whatever I can do."

"Can you tell us what you were doing last night?"

Durkin's eyes widened. "Wait...me?"

"Certainly," replied Bell, adjusting his napkin on his lap. "It's just a matter of elimination. We have to ask everyone."

"Oh, right. Of course. Well, it was my turn to close, so I locked up shortly after 11:00. Last night was kind of slow, so it didn't take long to get everyone out of here. I called my wife to let her know when I'd be home, and I pretty much went straight home."

"What time was that?"

"Around 11:15 or so. It doesn't take me long to get home. I arrived around 11:30."

"Will your wife corroborate that?"

"Of course. She was up watching TV Land. She loves all of those old sitcoms."

"When you don't close," Bell queried, "who does?"

"My assistant manager, Brandi. She was off last night, but she's working tonight. She's out on her break now. She's also scheduled to close tomorrow."

"Thanks. We'll make sure we get a hold of her and everyone else here, just to cover all the bases. Oh, one more thing. Among the effects we found in Kevin's wallet were some Dalia's Dollars. Do you know how often he frequented Dalia's Delights?"

Durkin looked sheepish. "I took him there, once, for his birthday. He'd seemed a bit down at the time, and I thought it might cheer him up. I paid for the whole thing."

35

"Was there any kind of trouble during your visit? Did he get into an argument with anyone? Piss off the management for his treatment of the girls? Anything you can think of?"

"No. If anything, he seemed a little embarrassed to be there. He was really shy most of the time."

Bell made a mental note to check it out anyway.

Nicole chimed in. "We know you said he didn't really have any friends outside of work, but if you can think of anyone he knew or was friendly with, that would be a great help."

As Durkin nodded, Bell added, "We have a team of officers coming to go over Kevin's apartment in a little while, so we request that no one enter the apartment."

A look of shock crossed Durkin's face. "Do you think it might have happened here?"

"We don't know," Bell replied, "but for now, we'll have to treat it as a crime scene. It's strictly procedure. No one is to go in or out unless authorized by the police until further notice." *And who knows how badly the scene's been contaminated already?*

Like all good detectives, Bell knew that the first hour after a crime is crucial when it comes to securing the scene. One of the most notorious cases in recent American history had been the murder of Nicole Brown Simpson and her friend Ron Goldman in 1994. Few precautions were taken by police at the scene in front of Simpson's home. Various police personnel had carelessly walked about, tracking blood and other trace evidence all over the place. The bodies had been left lying for ten hours before a medical examiner was called in, and even then he didn't do any examinations at the scene but bagged the bodies for a trip to the morgue, ignoring drops of blood on Nicole Simpson's back and ruining evidence that could have pinpointed a doer. No one had even bothered to photograph the interior of her home, which could have indicated whether there was a struggle inside that spilled to the outside. Basically, police ineptitude had led to accusations of evidence tampering and planting and, many believed, also to former football player O.J. Simpson (Nicole's estranged husband) getting away with murder. It was a classic case of what not to do when investigating a homicide.

In Bell's newest assignment, the scene where the body had been found had been secured properly, but Kevin Myers's apartment was another story entirely. According to Locard's Exchange Principle, any two surfaces coming into contact means trace evidence can be left behind. Both Bell and Nicole, as well as Durkin the landlord, had walked into the apartment with no protection over their shoes, which meant they had dragged in God knew what. They had had the foresight to put gloves on before touching anything. That and the fact that the apartment might not have actually been the crime scene were small comforts, especially considering what Sergeant Baker would likely have to say about it when he found out.

After the two detectives had eaten their meals, Bell caught the waitress's eye. She held up her index finger, indicating that she'd be there momentarily. Within a couple minutes, she joined them at their table, with a plateful of meatloaf and mashed potatoes in front of her. Nicole did her best not to look at the plate or catch a whiff of the meatloaf that would send her back to painful reminisces and set her stomach into hurricanes.

"Ya mind? It's the only chance I'll have for dinner," the waitress apologized.

"Not a problem, as long as you don't mind us asking you questions while you eat," Bell replied as Nicole readied her notepad. "What's your name?"

"Emma Watson." She poured a bit of ketchup on her meatloaf and ate with more gusto than either Bell or Nicole had.

Must be desensitized to the so-called food in this place, Nicole reflected somewhat sourly as her stomach rumbled. The clam chowder she'd eaten wasn't sitting very well. *Surprise, surprise. Well, I'll just have to deal with it.*

"How long have you been working here?"

"About five years. I used to work at Templeton's a few streets over, but I got tired of those fights breaking out between the customers." She smiled wanly. "Things here are a little more...calm and stable."

"How well did you know Kevin Myers?" Nicole queried.

"Oh, about as well as you can know the people you work with, I guess. He'd been working here about a year or so. He was a quiet guy, good worker. He was always ready to help anyone with anything. He was also very polite. Really, he reminds me of...er, reminded me of my brother Fred. I think the drill sergeants must've pounded politeness into Fred, because he sure wasn't that way when we were kids!"

"Kevin was in the Army," said Bell. "Did he ever talk about it?"

Emma's eyes widened in surprise. "No. Really? I had no idea." She pushed her mashed potatoes about with her fork. "Like I said, he didn't talk much, especially about himself. He was just really nice - nicer than a lot of people around here."

Bell's ears perked up. "What do you mean by that?"

"Nothing, really. It was just kind of unusual for a guy like him to be in a neighborhood like this." She tucked a stray lock of hair behind her left ear. "Say, why are you asking so many questions? He just got hit by a car, an accident, right?"

Bell glanced at Nicole, who took up the thread. "We're sorry, Emma, but it looks like Kevin was murdered. We need to find out as much as we can about him, his friends, and any problems he might have had recently."

Tears welled up in Emma's eyes. "Murdered? But who would want to kill Kevin? He wouldn't have hurt a fly."

"I know this must be difficult for you," Nicole said, "but really, anything you can tell us would be helpful. We really don't have much to go on at this point."

She and Bell waited while Emma wiped her eyes and blew her nose with her paper napkin. The plate, with its remnants of meatloaf and potatoes, was pushed aside, and a busboy came by to clear the table.

When the busboy had gone, Bell began again. "First, we have to ask you where you were last Friday night."

"Me?" she asked in astonishment.

"We have to ask everyone."

"I was here, working. I work every other Friday night from 3:00 until closing."

"Who else was here?"

"Let's see...Lori, Wanda, Heather – they're all waitresses. Mr. Durkin was here, of course. Daryl was in the kitchen and Lawrence was here, bussing and washing dishes. Kevin had the night off. He told me he just planned to relax in front of the TV with some snacks."

"You say he was nice, quiet, and a good worker. How did he interact with the rest of the staff?"

"Okay, I guess" Emma sniffed. "He wasn't real close to anyone, but he joked around with a couple of the guys. Sometimes they'd go out for a few drinks after we closed."

"Who?"

"Daryl and Lawrence. I don't think they were best friends or anything, but they seemed to get along pretty well. They're not here today, though. I think they'll be in tomorrow."

Nicole nodded to indicate that she'd noted the need to talk to Daryl and Lawrence as soon as possible.

Bell continued his line of questioning. "How about Mr. Durkin?"

Emma looked around. Once she saw that Durkin was occupied on the other side of the restaurant, she spoke in a lower tone. "Old Snowy?" When Bell and Nicole looked confused, she brushed her shoulders, and Nicole had to stifle a laugh. "I guess they got along fine. Durkin is a bit of a grump, but he's all right. He doesn't make the wait staff pool their tips like some other places, and he's pretty flexible with the scheduling. If you need time off, he'll do his best to help you out."

Bell thought about Durkin's wife. "Does Mrs. Durkin work here?"

Emma snorted. "That diva? She only comes in to ask her poor old hubby for money so she can go shopping. I doubt she's ever lifted a finger in her entire life, except to pile that makeup on her face."

"So you don't remember anything strange happening? Nothing that might have precipitated a problem between Kevin and anyone else here?"

"Not really." Emma wrinkled her forehead in thought. "Wait! Geez, I almost forgot. A couple of weeks ago, there were these guys in here for dinner. Kevin bumped into one of the other waitresses, and she spilled some drinks on them. They went absolutely berserk, calling Kevin every name in the book – real nasty stuff. It didn't matter that Kevin apologized all over the place. Nothing he said seemed to make a difference to these two. Like I said, there aren't a lot of nice guys in this neighborhood."

"What do you mean by that? What kind of real nasty stuff?"

Emma looked slightly uncomfortable. "They looked like a couple of skinheads - leather and chains, tattoos, the whole thing. They said some really vile things to Kevin."

Nicole broke in. "Did he respond in any way?"

"Not really, other than to keep apologizing. He seemed to take it pretty calmly, as was part of Kevin's laidback nature, but I think that only made them madder."

"So what happened?" Bell wondered.

"Durkin heard all the yelling and came out. He threatened to call the cops if they didn't leave right away. I guess they weren't as tough as they pretended to be, because they took off pretty fast. Some of our regulars were pretty upset by the whole ordeal."

"Had they been in before?"

"Maybe. I don't know. I don't think they've been in since."

"Would you recognize them if you saw them again?"

"I'm not sure."

"Would you be willing to look at some pictures down at the station?"

Emma twisted her finger in that lock of crinkly brown hair that had escaped her ponytail. "Well, I guess I could. Do you think they might have something to do with what happened to Kevin?"

"We don't know anything at this point," Bell said. "We're pretty much at square one. Whatever you could do to help would really be appreciated."

"Okay." Emma smiled weakly. "I really liked Kevin, and I want to help if I can." After Bell gave her information on where to go and what to do, she stood and gathered her plate. "I gotta get back to work. Can you tell me when you find the creep who did this?"

"Of course," Nicole said gently. "Thank you, Emma, and we may have other questions for you down the road, if that's okay."

Emma nodded and moved on.

Nicole watched after her for a moment, then looked back at Bell.

"What do you think? Skinheads?"

"Who knows?" Bell sighed. "If they were jacked up on something and were pissed off enough, they might have." *If it was Skinheads on some quest for making a racial statement*, Bell thought, *they wouldn't have bothered with killing Kevin in such a relatively peaceful way, and they certainly wouldn't have bothered staging an accident to cover it up. Those assholes want to be seen and heard. They would have jumped him, pummeled him, and, if murder was on their minds, knifed or shot him in plain sight.* Still, he knew the lead would have to be followed. Strange things happened all the time in the world of homicide.

While the two detectives were in Durkin's, the Crime Scene Unit had descended upon the upstairs apartment. The entrance had been taped off, and an officer had been assigned to monitor all comings and goings of approved visitors. Carpet fiber samples were collected, along with fiber samples from the unmade bed. While some dusted for fingerprints, others snapped innumerable photos.

Bell and Nicole arrived and stood to the side, watching the hive of activity silently.

Simon Cleary, a tall man with wavy blond hair and a rumpled look about him, approached.

"What's new, Simon?" Bell asked.

"Not much," Simon replied. "We're combing the place for the usual samples, but so far nothing is jumping out at me - no visible blood, no obvious bodily fluids. I'm afraid I won't really have any news for you tonight."

"Crap. Well, let us know right away if you find anything meaningful." Bell looked at his watch. He and Nicole had both been up most of the night because it was their turn on the night shift, and they had also both gotten up early to pursue the few leads they had in the case. "Come on," he said to Nicole." "We might as well head home. It'll be another long day for us tomorrow." He looked at her closely. She seemed paler than usual, and there were dark circles under her eyes.

"Hey, are you okay?"

"I'm fine," she said quickly, noting the hint of real concern in his voice. "Like you said, it's been a long day. I just need a shower and a good night's sleep. Let's go."

Chapter Four

When Bell got back to his apartment, he changed into a t-shirt and boxers for bed and saw that his answering machine was blinking. He groaned softly when he heard his mother's voice coming out of the playback messages.

"Hello, John! It's Mother, just checking up on you. Please give me a call as soon as you can. Toodle-doo!"

Bell looked at the clock. It was 10:00 p.m. *Ha,* he thought, *No respectable son would call his mother at this late hour, now would he?* He was glad to be off the hook – pun intended – for the time being. Most of his important calls came through on his cell phone, but he had so far refused to give the number to his mother, using the excuse that it was only for work purposes. She was so wrapped up in her own affairs that she didn't question his reasoning. Tired but too wired to go to bed just yet, he pulled a bottle of beer out of the fridge and plopped down in front of the television. He flipped through the channels and finally stopped at the History Channel, which was showing yet another documentary on the ancient secrets of Egypt. Half-listening to Secretary General of the Egyptian Supreme Council of Antiquities Zahi Hawass – who always managed to get his mug on all the documentaries about ancient Egypt and even now had his very own show called *"Chasing Mummies"* – blathering on about some new discovery in the Valley of the Kings, he idly thought about his relationship with his parents.

Like many others he knew, Bell was the product of a working class family. His father had worked long hours at the Budd Company Red Lion plant building railway cars, trying to provide a good life for his family. Long hours during the week meant Peter Bell was often too tired on the weekends to spend much time with his son. For many years, Bell had harbored a smoldering resentment that dad didn't often do things like play ball or go on Cub Scout campouts, but as he got older and began his own career – one that posed many demands on his time and his sanity – his resentment faded to a grudging acceptance and understanding of his father that he hadn't known very well as a child. Plus, it was gratifying to know from things he heard from his aunts and uncles that dad was really proud of his accomplishments. So while Bell's relationship with his father was not as close as it might have been, he got along well enough with him as an adult.

His mother was a different story.

Jeanette Bell was one of those women who was never happy unless she was managing other people's lives. Always busy in groups like the PTA and the local chapter of the Junior Women's Club, she was forever organizing fundraisers and other charitable events, leaving little time for involvement in her own son's activities. Often left to fend for himself, Bell had become self-sufficient to the point that he now resented any attempt by his mother to "get a little closer." It was as if she suddenly remembered that she had a son whose life she thought could use her organizing influence. When Renee had broken up with him, his mother had almost been more devastated than he was. *Likely because she had seen herself in a pivotal role in the wedding planning,* he thought sourly, pulling on his beer. Yes, he knew she loved him, and he loved her as a dutiful son should but that didn't necessarily make interacting with her much easier or more enjoyable, especially when she was constantly asking him if he and Renee had managed to patch things up. Fortunately, his job made it so that he couldn't manage more than the occasional dinner, and he even had to miss out on some holiday gatherings. *Darn. Sorry, Mom,* he mused, chugging another gulp.

Ah yes, his job. That had been another sticking point with dear old Mom. His mother had always thought he was destined to become a lawyer or a stockbroker – something she could brag about to the likeminded women with whom she spent most of her waking hours. *"My son says to buy gold,"* she'd be able to tell them conspiratorially. When he announced his intention to enter the lowly police force, she'd thought he was kidding. When she finally figured out he wasn't joking, her amusement had turned into bitter disbelief.

"Really, John, sometimes I don't think I even know you," she'd said sadly. *No kidding,* he'd thought, but he'd managed to keep his mouth shut.

His thoughts drifted back to Renee Anderson. Even though he was slowly getting over the pain of the breakup, thinking about her still gave him an unhappy twinge. The two of them had met at a party given by mutual friends and had hit it off immediately. Bell remembered being drawn to her quick and ready laugh, as well as her natural, almost casual blonde beauty. And there was no denying that the woman had been dynamite in bed. But the relationship that had started out as a welcome diversion from the everyday horrors of his job eventually deteriorated because Renee was unable to cope with that job's demands. A dental hygienist, she herself only worked four days a week and always had plenty of time for recreation in the evenings and on weekends – a luxury Bell certainly didn't have, especially when he was working a case.

Also, unfortunately, she was emotionally needy. While Bell's childhood had created a self-reliant, self-contained boy and man, Renee had grown up in the wake of her parents' constant bickering and fighting. Rather than get divorced, Bell's would-have-been-in-laws stayed together "for the children," and Renee and her siblings learned how to play one parent off the other to get what they wanted. Bell might not have had a close relationship with his parents while growing up, but they were happy enough in their own way and had never used him against each other in petty feuds. For that, he was thankful, especially after seeing the end result of such poor parenting in Renee.

When Renee eventually realized that Bell wasn't going to sacrifice his career for her social needs, she pouted at first, and then she tried to make him jealous by shamelessly flirting with other men. When that didn't work, she began arguing with him over what Bell considered trivial things, like his not being able to escort her to a party because he was on duty or bitching that sometimes he was too tired to fully enjoy some activity she had planned for them. No matter how often he tried to explain his wacky schedule and the toll it would take on any normal human being, Renee never seemed to understand. He certainly didn't try to prevent her from going to events without him; he wasn't the possessive type, and wanted her to have a good time even if he couldn't be there. Eventually, however, Renee decided that she'd rather have a good time with someone else, and she promptly dumped Bell for the kind of guy who shaved his chest and got regular manicures, a guy who worked at an ad agency and used words like "fabulous" in every other sentence.

At the time, Nicole – always a good one to lend an ear – had sympathized, but she'd also tried to explain that if he had really wanted that particular relationship to work, he should have tried a little harder to make Renee feel special. But what Bell needed in a relationship was a partner, an equal, someone who would always back him up but not crowd him. Neither his job nor his personality was suited for a clingy whiner. *Nope. The ad exec can have her,* he thought, taking his third gulp. *I'm sure they're fabulous together.* Nevertheless, hindsight didn't necessarily lessen the sting or the shock of the breakup, especially since he hadn't seen it coming. Again, in the aftermath, Nicole had pointed out a number of clues he should have caught on to but hadn't.

Grimacing, Bell drained the beer bottle, ran his hand through his short, dark hair and hit the mute button in the middle of one of Zahi Hawass's self-serving speeches about dead Egyptian royalty. *Screw Renee and her ad exec.* Kevin Myers, the poor bastard, was lying cold on a slab awaiting official identification from bereaved relatives who were on their way north from

Georgia. So far, there was little to go on: He'd been in the Army, but for how long was anyone's guess; he'd worked at a crummy job in a greasy spoon; and while he seemed to have few close relationships, he was generally liked by those who knew him. They were no closer to discovering why he was found under a stolen car in a different neighborhood in what appeared to be a phony accident than they had been when the bookstore woman first found him wedged there. And now, the possibility of skinheads had come into the picture. *Skinheads? When will that particularly revolting racist group finally die out?* Bell realized that like most other radical fringe groups, they were usually down on their luck and blamed their unfortunate lot in life on someone else – in this case, black people. *But then*, Bell thought, *racism goes on in various segments of society, and people of all colors and creeds are subjected to degradations of every variety. It certainly isn't the prerogative of snotty white kids with gigantic chips on their shoulders. So much for that dream of yours, Dr. King.*

Clicking the television off, Bell decided to head to bed. He knew the next day, there'd be alibis to check and other avenues of inquiry to follow. Right now, bed sounded infinitely preferable to wallowing in self-pity.

The next day promised to be a bright and cheery one, but Bell was in no mood for lollipops and rainbows. He hadn't slept well, and the fact that he got caught on the phone with his mother for half an hour had only made his mood that much blacker. She wanted to know if he could stop by soon for dinner and a nice long chat about what was going on in his life. Fortunately, he was able to stave her off with the excuse that he was in the middle of a hot homicide case and wouldn't have much free time for a while. It was a temporary remedy, however; she was a persistent woman, and he knew in the end he'd have to give in eventually. *Anyway*, he reasoned, trying to sugarcoat the idea, *it would be nice to see Dad...and my parents aren't getting any younger.*

Slumping into the Homicide office, he found his usual desk empty and made a beeline for it. He tossed his jacket on the back of his chair, and sat down. There, bigger than life, was the Sunday edition of *The Inquirer*, the headline screaming "Murder in Kensington Baffles Philly PD" in a ridiculously large and bold font. Sucking in his breath sharply, he scanned the article. Fortunately, it was just a layout of the few facts Jean Gardner had been able to weasel out of Nicole, accompanied by the usual veiled inference that the cops were an incompetent lot of knuckle-draggers. He tossed the paper aside and looked up to see Nicole beaming down at him.

"Sleep well?" she asked.

He scowled in return, but she just laughed.

"Come on. Get over yourself. It's a gorgeous day today."

"BFD," he said, but he smiled in spite of himself.

Nicole's cheer was infectious. What he didn't know was that the cheer was forced. She'd woken up heaving and had made a dash for the bathroom. For now, her stomach was settled. What was not settled was how she was going to break the news to her husband and the rest of her family. The news should have been joyful, an occasion for cigars and pink and blue balloons with images of infant-bearing storks on them, but instead, it was giving her paroxysms of dread.

The two detectives spent the next hour or so making phone calls, as well as filling out the interminable paperwork that is part of any bureaucracy. When Bell spoke to Simon Cleary about the forensics sweep of Kevin Myers's apartment, he wasn't surprised to hear that there was no news yet as to what their search would yield. "You'll be the first to know," Simon promised.

As expected, they also received a number of calls prompted by Jean Gardner's newspaper story. Also as expected, most of the calls were from likely cranks who had nothing better to do than to waste the valuable time of law enforcement, but they'd have to follow up on each and every one, no matter how ludicrous, on the off chance that it was a valuable clue. Bell recalled one such idiot whose call he had been unfortunate enough to answer a couple years back.

"Okay, ma'am, I can check the warrant status in the computer," Bell had told her "What's the person's name?"

"I don't know."

"Um, okay. Well, what information do you have?"

"A friend of my friend is on the run. She lives at 10th and Godfrey."

"Do you know the exact address?"

"I already told you that, mister. I said 10th and Godfrey!"

"Uh, all right, does she live in the intersection, ma'am?"

"Are you crazy? No! She lives in a house there," she said in an annoyed tone of voice.

"Okay." Bell sighed. "What else do you have?"

"That's it."

"So, you called to report your friend's friend is on the run and lives in the area of 10th and Godfrey? What does she look like?"

"She's a black female."

"Do you have anything more specific? It's a primarily black neighborhood, ma'am, and there are a lot of females who live there."

"She's about average height. That's pretty much it."

"Okay, ma'am. We'll get right on it."

"Thanks!"

As he remembered the call, Bell once again realized they weren't paying him enough. He sighed and picked up the phone when it jingled. "Homicide. Detective Bell."

"Uh, yeah...um, I'm calling about that guy, the one who worked at the restaurant." The voice on the other end wavered just a little bit.

"What guy? What restaurant?" Bell wasn't going to give a potential crank caller any ammo to further waste his time.

"Kevin. He worked at Durkin's. I know something that might be helpful." Bell grabbed a pad and pencil.

Her voice wavered some more. "I dunno know if I should say anything."

"Ma'am..." Bell worked to keep his voice smooth and calm. "Kevin Myers was murdered. I can assure you that anything you tell us will be kept strictly confidential."

After a slight pause, the caller continued, "Well, okay. I think his boss did it."

"His boss? Reginald Durkin?"

"Yeah."

After a few moments, Bell prompted. "What makes you think that, ma'am?"

"Look, I happen to know that Durkin hires guys under the table. I think Kevin knew and was going to rat him out to the IRS, so Durkin killed him to shut him up."

Bell had to work to keep the skepticism out of his voice. "How do you know all of this exactly? Do you have proof?"

"No. It's just a theory."

"We don't deal in theories. We need facts. Could I have your name?" But all Bell received in reply was a sharp *click*, followed by a dial tone. He tossed his pencil down and slumped down in his chair, a movement that caught Nicole's eye.

"Any luck?" she queried. Bell quickly related the gist of the short phone conversation. "No name, eh? Sounds like either a former employee or someone who didn't get hired, somebody who has an axe to grind with Durkin. Still, I suppose we'll have to check it out."

"I suppose so." Bell grimaced. "Any luck in tracking down information about Myers's Army stint?"

"Not yet. I'm hoping the local recruiter can look him up for us, but the office is closed until tomorrow. I did get a call about that skinhead incident Emma told us about yesterday though. There might be something more to that than meets the eye."

"I don't suppose there were any more salient details, such as where the punks live."

"No-o-o." Nicole tapped her pad with her pen. "But the guy did know where they hang out." She rattled off an address.

"What are we waiting for?" Bell grabbed his jacket. "Let's take a ride out there and see what's what."

A short while later, the detectives found themselves in the Frankford section of the city. Located in the lower northeast section of Philadelphia, roughly bounded by the original run of Frankford Creek, the area is known for its manufacturing history. Aramingo Mills, once a principal manufacturer of dry goods, was now vacant, and the building was deteriorating. The Franklin Woolen Mill, which first opened its doors in 1827, now housed an auto repair business. Globe Dye Works, located on the corner of Torresdale Avenue and Kinsey Street, had closed its doors in 2005 after having been run by five generations of the Greenwood family.

The former Frankford Arsenal was also located there. It was now home to the Arsenal Business Center, which housed a candy manufacturer, several charter schools, and a catering company – not to mention headquarters for several Philadelphia Police Department divisions: City Wide Vice Enforcement, Dignitary Protection and the Narcotics Strike Force. The arsenal's most recent claim to fame was that it served as a filming location for several well-known Hollywood movies, including *"Philadelphia," "Twelve Monkeys"* and *"Fallen."*

Historically, Frankford had had an "unofficial" division among racial lines, Frankford Avenue separating the whites in Frankford proper from the blacks in East Frankford. That distinction seemed to have disappeared in modern times, but unfortunately, gangs were rife in the neighborhood, and both Bell and Nicole could imagine a group of skinheads fitting in quite nicely amongst the other deviants. Making their way to the 4300 block of Disston Street, they scanned the rows of somewhat shabby two-story brick twins with small front porches before getting out of the car and making their way to the address supplied by the tipster. The small front yard was choked with weeds and littered with debris, including beer bottles and countless cigarette butts, and the paint on the door and around the window frames – which had once been white but now a grayish brown – was peeling.

With his gun securely tucked into its holster and his ID in hand, Bell marched up to the weathered front door, Nicole hard on his heels. After discovering that the doorbell didn't seem to work, he knocked loudly. After a few moments of silence, he banged again. Still nothing. A peek in the window was fruitless, as the tattered Venetian blind, coupled with filth on the glass, obscured the view. Nicole jerked her head toward the adjoining house, where they could see an older woman peeping out of her window. They promptly crossed over and, flashing their badges, rapped on the door. The woman, with her short white hair, wrinkled visage, and pink cardigan over a flowered housedress looked like she could be anywhere between sixty and ninety, squinted at the badges before slowly opening the door. For a moment, Nicole had a vision of that cranky cartoon character from the greeting cards and she had to stifle a laugh.

"What's the problem?" Her voice was low and raspy, as if she'd been smoking unfiltered cigarettes all of her life.

"No problem." Nicole took the lead, smiling. "I'm Detective Ellis, and this is Detective Bell. We'd just like to ask you some questions about your neighbors. Do you have a few minutes? It won't take long."

"Sure, why not? There's nothing good on the tube anyway." She headed toward the small living room, her dark blue slippers shuffling on the worn brown carpeting. Her home was shabby but clean, and the smell of stale cigarette smoke lingered in the air. A small television set was situated in the corner of the living room, and the woman clicked it off. Indicating that they should sit on the small settee, she herself sat down in a matching armchair facing them.

Nicole whipped out her notebook.

"Mrs…?"

"Jacobson. Ellie Jacobson."

"Mrs. Jacobson-"

"Call me Ellie."

"Okay, thank you. Ellie, we're trying to find out as much as we can about the people who live in the twin next door. Can you tell us anything?"

Ellie snorted. "Not much to tell." She fished a pack of cigarettes out of her dress pocket and lit one with a cheap, disposable lighter, inhaling as though she was tasting the nectar of the gods. "Doctor says I gotta quit," she explained, "but at my age, who cares? I'm gonna die at some point, right? Said he could get me some of those patches or that gum, but I'd probably try to light that up and smoke it too! Anyway, you didn't come to hear about my bad habits. You came to ask about the folks next door. Who's in trouble?"

"No one," Bell replied. "We're actually just looking for them because we want to ask them a few questions." He could tell Nicole was bothered by the woman's smoking, but as a former smoker who sometimes missed the habit, he was almost enjoying it, living vicariously through the inhalations.

"Humph. Up to no good, I'm sure. The house next door is owned by Margie Hendricks, but she's in a nursing home now. I dunno if she's gonna make it back home or not. We've been neighbors and friends since we both moved here, back when we was newlyweds. We've both outlived our husbands, and we looked out for each other until she couldn't take care of herself anymore." Quickly swiping her hand over her eyes, she continued. "Her no-good grandson stays there now. That boy's a real piece of work. And those friends of his! I wouldn't put anything past that rotten bunch." She took a deep drag of her cigarette and exhaled slowly.

"What's his name, this grandson?" Nicole's pencil was poised for action.

"Drew Nichols. His mother Jane, is Margie's daughter. Margie has two children, Jane and Richard. Richard is an accountant. He lives in Jersey with his wife and children - such a lovely man and a lovely family too. They always stop in to say hello whenever they're down for a visit. But that Jane, she always had a real wild streak in her. Poor Margie tried, but she was no match for that girl's hard head. Jane ended up marrying a real loser. He left her after a while, took off to God knows where, so she and Drew moved back in with Margie when Drew was just a few years old. Phil Hendricks, Margie's husband, was already dead by then – cancer – and poor Margie was lonely. I think she probably regretted taking Jane and Drew in, but what can you do? We gotta stick by blood. Although I have to say, sometimes you should just cut your losses." Her voice had a ring of conviction that seemed to speak of firsthand experience.

Bell leaned forward, placing his hands on his knees. "Where's Jane now?"

"Jail. Busted for too many DUIs." Ellie sighed. "I think she'll be out in a few months though."

It was a sad story that was all too familiar, Bell reflected. A deadbeat dad takes off and leaves the wife and children to fend for themselves. Then the children, often boys, who grow up in such circumstances often feel abandoned and neglected, and sometimes lashed out against society by some sort of rebellion. He knew a high percentage of young men with violent, antisocial tendencies, including those in gangs, came from fatherless homes, and it certainly didn't help when the mother had issues as well. If Drew Nichols was really as wild as Ellie Jacobson was intimating, his family situation could be playing a serious role, but Bell wasn't in the business of sorting out the psychological aspects of crime. He only cared about one thing: finding out who committed murder – in this case, who killed Kevin Myers. He'd leave the social implications to the shrinks.

Nicole was jotting down notes as quickly as she could. "You said Drew is staying here. Do you know if he has a job?"

"I have no idea. If he does, he must work really odd hours." Ellie stubbed out her cigarette in a pink plastic ashtray that was already close to overflowing. "He's in and out at all hours of the day. When Margie left for the home, Drew began having all sorts of wild parties - sometimes during the day, sometimes at night. I didn't let that go on for too long, let me tell you. Had to call the cops a couple of times before he got the message that I wasn't going to put up with it. Now and again, he'll have a few friends over, but it's nothing like before." She paused for a moment. "You said you want to ask him and his friends a few questions. Do you mind if I ask what about?"

"We're hoping they might be able to help us regarding a case we're working on. Really, we just have a few routine questions for him. Is there anything else you can tell us? Maybe about his friends?"

"What's to tell? Honestly, they're a bunch of bums. I wouldn't be surprised if not a one of them works. Who'd hire such hooligans, anyway? They'd scare off the customers. Most of them have shaved heads, tattoos, and wear combat boots, even in the summer! I don't usually see many girls around, although the one or two I have seen are a pretty sorry lot."

Ellie suddenly leaned forward, a frown wrinkling her brow. "Look, I'm no dummy. If it involves Drew and his crowd, I'm sure it can't be good. Does he have to know you were here? I mean, I can take care of myself, but..." She looked down, twisting the hem of her housedress in her hands.

"Not to worry," Bell assured her. "We received the tip from someone else - a couple people, actually. He certainly doesn't have to know we spoke to you. Look, we have to go now. Any idea when a good time to come back would be?"

"It's hard to say for sure, but he's usually around in the afternoon - sometimes alone, sometimes not."

"Fine. We'll come back then." Bell nodded to Nicole, and they both rose from the settee. Bell handed the elderly woman a card. "If you have any questions for us, or if something happens that you think we might need to know about, please call anytime."

Ellie studied the card. "Homicide?" She sucked in her breath. "Did Drew *kill* someone? He's a troublemaker, yes, but I would never have dreamt he'd-"

"Not that we're aware." Bell gave Nicole a quick sideways glance. "We're just hoping he can shed some light on a case we're working on." After saying goodbye, they let themselves out and made their way back to the unmarked car. They sat inside for a few moments, quietly going over their personal impressions. Nicole was the first to speak.

"She's scared of him."

"Can you blame her? He sounds like a real winner."

"If he doesn't have a job, I wonder how he supports himself."

"Drugs maybe. Who knows? Or maybe he's on the up and up and just collects unemployment like so many other upstanding citizens." Bell looked at his watch. "Come on. We have time to talk to Durkin's wife before lunch, and we're going to have to follow up on that illegal alien tip."

Ellie watched them drive away, and she shivered slightly, pulling her cardigan around her a bit more tightly. Sitting down on the couch, she thought about her neighbors. Drew had been a sweet little boy, but his mother's antics, combined with the lack of a father figure and too much time on his hands after school, meant he had inevitably fallen in with the wrong crowd and it was all downhill from there. The idea that Margie's grandson could have turned out so badly was heartbreaking to Ellie, but there was little to be done about it now.

She hadn't told the detectives, but she'd overheard some frightful fighting next door on a few occasions. She knew Drew's girlfriend lived with him and that she was usually the focus of his rages. Ellie had tried talking to her about it when Drew wasn't home, but she was told by the girl to "mind your own fucking business, you old bitch." That was the first and last time she'd tried to intervene. Knowing full well that Drew's temper could easily turn on her, despite her having been kind to him when he was a child, she didn't feel safe intervening. She hoped the two nice detectives would keep their word and not mention her name.

Her eyes misted over. *What is the world coming to? When I was that age, no self-respecting young woman would even think of moving in with a man she wasn't married to, let alone someone of Drew's ilk. But today, it seemed, anything goes. Sexual promiscuity is no longer frowned upon but egged on by popular culture, and young people no longer even seem to respect their bodies, what with all the tattooing and piercing they flaunt around here every day.*

    She turned the television on again and flipped through the channels until she came upon an *"I Love Lucy"* rerun. She sank back into the cushions and stared at the screen. Sometimes it was just better to think about how it used to be rather than how it was now.

Chapter Five

Reginald Durkin and his wife lived just a few blocks away from the diner in a town house on Catharine Street. It was much nicer than some of the others in the neighborhood, sporting a white stucco exterior, a covered porch and a flower box at the window.

As he knocked on the door, Bell could hear the television blaring, and it took a minute or two for the door to open.

"Yes?"

"Mrs. Durkin?"

"Yes?" Her eyebrows drew together in puzzlement. "What can I do for you?"

"I'm Detective Bell, and this is Detective Ellis." They displayed their badges, waiting until she nodded in understanding before putting them away. "We're just here as a formality regarding the Kevin Myers case. May we come in?"

She frowned slightly. "Reginald isn't here. You'll find him at the restaurant."

"It's you we've come to talk to."

"Oh, of course. Please, right this way." They followed Mrs. Durkin into a pleasant living room, where an elliptical trainer stood in one corner. The inside of the house was just as attractive as the outside, and it was apparent that a lot of work had been done to improve it over the years. Mrs. Durkin grabbed a nearby towel and wiped her brow and neck. "I was just exercising. Gotta keep firming the flab." Tucking her hair behind her ears, she invited them to sit down on a couch near the window. "May I get you a drink? Coffee?" When they shook their heads, she upped the ante. "How about some water or fruit juice?"

"No thank you, Mrs. Durkin. We just-" Bell began.

"Alice. Please call me Alice. I don't prefer to stand on ceremony." She sat in one of two comfortable-looking armchairs opposite the couch.

"Okay, Alice. Thank you, but we don't intend to stay long. We just need to verify your husband's whereabouts on the night of Kevin Myers's death."

Her left hand rose to her throat. "Is he a suspect?"

"Everyone's a suspect in a murder investigation, at least in the beginning. But this is really just a formality. Confirming alibis helps us in our process of elimination." He looked at Nicole.

Consulting her notes, Nicole picked up the thread. "According to your husband, he was scheduled to close the restaurant that night. He locked up at about 11:15 and arrived home around 11:30." She cocked her head to one side. "Would you say that's accurate?"

"Let's see. That was what, Friday night? Yes. It was his turn to close the restaurant. He and Brandi, his assistant manager, take turns. The restaurant closes by 11:00, and it doesn't take long for things to get wrapped up and for him to get home. It's only a few blocks away."

"Can you tell us what you were doing when he got here?"

"Oh, I was up watching television. I don't like to go to bed until Reginald gets home. I can't sleep until I know he's home safe. There's so much crime these days."

"We know," Bell said ruefully.

Alice looked stricken. "I didn't mean to sound insensitive. I-"

"It's all right, Mrs...er, Alice. We know what you meant," Nicole said smoothly. "Please go on. You said you were waiting up, watching television?"

"Yes, that's right. I love to watch the old sitcoms on TV Land. They were having a *Three's Company* marathon that night. I just love that show, especially the early episodes, the ones with the Ropers."

"Are you sure about the time your husband arrived home? That is very important."

"Positive. He showed up just when one episode ended and another one began. Plus, I have a habit of looking at the clock on the cable box when he comes in."

Bell thought about the timetable. The M.E. on the scene estimated the time of death somewhere between 8:00 and 11:00 that night, and Dr. Barnes had agreed with that estimate during the autopsy. Durkin was at the restaurant because it was his turn to lock up, and one of his employees, Emma, had vouched for his presence there that night. So unless he had a transporter like in *'Star Trek,'* it didn't seem possible that he was the murderer.

"How about you? How well did you know Kevin?"

"Not very well. I don't spend a lot of time at the restaurant. I don't really know the employees, except to say hello."

"So you don't work at Durkin's?" Bell pressed.

"Not anymore. I did in the beginning, but once things got underway, Reggie hired a proper assistant manager."

Nicole arched her eyebrows at that. The parents of one of her close friends from high school owned a restaurant, and from Nicole's understanding of the business, restaurants were usually family affairs; it was hard work, and everyone pitched in. It seemed odd that Alice Durkin seemed to have no involvement whatsoever. Emma had called her a "diva." Nicole thought perhaps there was some truth to that label, especially as she glanced around the room. The Durkins' home was tastefully decorated in modern contemporary style, and the living room was painted a pale shade of yellow and sported a number of stylish prints and ornamental bric-a-brac. A well-stocked bar dominated one corner of the room, personal home bars having become trendy again. It reminded Nicole of the homes in one of those home magazines — everything perfect, everything expensive, and probably picked out by a professional who charged out the wazoo.

Alice also seemed to be a somewhat high-maintenance person, at least by appearances. She was a woman somewhere in her mid-fifties, her stylish mid-length bob was professionally highlighted, and her efforts on the elliptical trainer had obviously paid some handsome dividends. Nicole wondered if she'd had a boob job. The skin under her eyes looked a bit puffy though. She wore a wedding band and an engagement ring with a fairly large diamond, which she was now twisting about nervously on her finger. Her workout sneakers didn't look cheap either. Alice Durkin was obviously used to very nice things, but she and her husband seemed an odd pair. *Oh well. There's no accounting for attraction.*

Nicole was brought out of her musings as Bell continued the line of questioning, and she continued to scribble in her notebook.

"Well, even if you didn't know Kevin, surely your husband talks about work. Did he mention any problems that Kevin might have had? Issues with any of the staff?"

Alice pursed her lips in thought. "I don't think so. I can't think of anything. Things seemed to be going pretty well. Most of the staff has been there for quite a while. I think there are some new guys in the kitchen, but like I said, I don't know enough about it to comment."

"How about the business in general? Good? Bad? Any difficulties?"

"No problems, to my knowledge." Her finely shaped brows drew together slightly. "Why should there be?"

Bell gave her his famous smile, guaranteed to melt most women's hearts, and it seemed to work its usual charm with Alice Durkin, as she visibly relaxed. "No reason at all. We're just trying to get as much background as possible. You wouldn't believe it, but some of the most mundane information can suddenly become important in a murder investigation."

"You know, now that you mention it, Reggie did mention that a couple of toughs had given Kevin a hard time a couple of weeks ago. He was going to call the cops on them, but they left before it came to that."

"Ah, yes, we're following up on that lead. Are you sure you can't think of anything else? Anything your husband might have mentioned?"

"No. I'm sorry I can't tell you more."

"Nonsense. You've been very helpful." They rose to go and as with Ellie Jacobson, gave her their cards in case she remembered anything, anything at all. They were out on the sidewalk a few moments later.

"Well, his alibi seems to pan out."

"True, but I thought she seemed a bit nervous."

Bell looked surprised. "What do you mean? She seemed pretty calm to me - much calmer than I'd be if I was being questioned about the death of one of my spouse's employees."

"She kept twisting her ring around her finger. I don't know. Maybe it's just a nervous habit she has. Emma might have been right about her being somewhat of a diva. What kind of person doesn't take an interest in the family business? And her tastes seem to run toward the expensive side. I felt like I'd stepped into an edition of *Martha Stewart Living*."

Bell yawned, still tired from the past couple of days. "So she's full of herself. I know plenty of people like that."

Nicole shrugged. "You're probably right. Where to now?"

"How about some lunch? Then we can go back to see if Drew has managed to stagger home from his night of partying or whatever he's been up to."

After they'd eaten at one of their favorite sandwich shops (with Nicole, like most women, swearing that she was eating way too much as she gobbled down her ham and cheese on rye), they returned to the home on Disston Street, the current residence of Drew Nichols. As they approached the front door, navigating round the labyrinth of trash in the yard, they noticed that Ellie Jacobson had closed her curtains. Some kind of screeching music could be heard faintly through the door, so Bell knocked loudly.

A few minutes passed, and no one answered. Irritated, Bell banged on the door with his fist. Finally, after they'd waited several minutes more, the door was jerked open. Standing there was a young woman with more attitude than a professional wrestler. She sported short, spiky, bleach-blonde hair and wore a tight t-shirt that said "Bitchy" across her small breasts. She completed the ensemble with ripped jeans that looked like they'd been painted on.

"Yeah?"

"Is Drew around?"

"Who wants to know?" She looked them both over with a scowl.

Bell was wearing clean, pressed khakis and a button-down blue shirt. Nicole, whose blonde hair was swept up in a loose chignon, wearing dressed professionally in pinstriped pants, a crisp white blouse, and low black pumps.

"What is this, the fashion police?" she sneered.

"No, just the regular police." Bell flashed his badge. "Where's Drew?"

Her eyes widened, and she shielded them with her hand.

Bell noticed that her pupils seemed slightly dilated, but they were from Homicide, not Narcotics. "Well?" His voice began to show a touch of impatience, which he was trying very hard to conceal.

"Um, he's inside," she mumbled, looking down at her bare, dirty feet.

"Great. Why don't you show us in?"

Standing aside, the girl made room for Bell and Nicole to pass. By design, the house was a mirror image of the Jacobson home next door, but unlike that house, it had been trashed. Nicole thought about Drew's grandmother, Margie Hendricks, and how she might be horrified to know what had happened to the love nest she'd first moved to as a young bride. As they moved further inside, a young man stumbled out of the kitchen demanding, "Mandy, who is it?" He stopped short when he saw that the visitors had already entered. "What the fuck, Mandy? Who the hell are these people?"

Drew Nichols looked like a stereotypical skinhead: black hair shaved close to the scalp and a few tattoos visible on his arms and neck. His build was slight but wiry, and his blue eyes were bloodshot. He glared at the two detectives standing in front of him. "What the hell do you want?"

Mandy had moved next to him and was tugging on his sleeve. "Drew, it's the cops," she said, almost pleadingly.

He shook her off.

"Listen, if that old bag next door has been complaining again, she can suck it. I haven't had any parties since the last time you guys were here." He slowly looked Nicole over. "Although I don't think you were with those assholes before. I think I'd remember you."

Hearing his shameless flirtations, Mandy rushed toward the stairs in a huff and stomped up them, slamming a door on the second floor.

Nicole gave Drew a cool glance that Bell recognized at once; he knew he'd better defuse the situation quickly.

"I think your girlfriend's upset, sonny," Nicole said.

"Sonny, is it? I could show you a thing or two, and – you wouldn't be calling me 'sonny' then." He licked his lips.

"Okay, that's enough." Bell grabbed Drew by the shirt and threw him toward the living room, which was littered with takeout containers, paper coffee cups, and a variety of other smelly debris. Dust thickly coated all of the surfaces that weren't otherwise covered with garbage.

"John-," Nicole started.

"Hey, fuck you! I should complain about police brutality," Drew shouted.

"Police brutality my ass. Now sit down." When Bell used that tone, most people complied.

Drew was no exception. He lowered himself onto a dirty, frayed armchair. Bell and Nicole moved in front of him, but stayed on their feet.

"What is this, the Spanish Inquisition or something?"

"Yeah, and you didn't expect it, did you? Look, we just want to ask you a few questions about an incident in Durkin's Restaurant a couple weeks back. Apparently, there was an altercation between you and one of the employees."

Drew sneered and lit a cigarette, blowing the smoke toward them. "Christ, you guys are slow on the uptake. Like you said, it was a couple weeks ago. Who the fuck cares now?"

"We do. Tell us what happened."

"No big deal. Some stupid nigger spilled a tray of drinks on me and my friends, so I told his clumsy ass off. It was no less than he deserved."

"Oh? And what did he really deserve?" Bell noticed some literature on a table next to Drew's chair from Stormfront, a white nationalist group.

"What they all deserve - to get the fuck out. We don't want them here."

"And what, exactly, would you be willing to do to achieve that?"

"What's that supposed to mean?" Drew squinted up at them, shifting in his chair. "Hey, wait a minute. I don't like where this is goin'. I told the nigger what a piece of shit he was, and then my friends and me left after the manager threatened to call the police. That's it. You got nothin' on me, man."

Bell's tone was grim. "What would make you think we have anything on you anyway?"

"Nothin'." He folded his arms over his chest, leaving his cigarette dangling precariously from his mouth.

"Did you know that guy who accidentally spilled drinks on you is now dead?"

Drew's eyes widened slightly, but he shook his head.

"Are you sure you and your pals didn't decide to go back and give him what you thought he, uh, deserved...what *you* thought he had coming to him?"

"No!"

"Where were you Friday night?"

"That's none of your damn business."

Bell leaned down, until his face was just inches from Drew's. He grabbed him by the shirt again. "Wrong. This is a murder investigation. Everything's our business. And if you want to keep your skinny little ass out of jail, you'll tell us what you were doing Friday night between 8:00 p.m. and midnight."

Crushing his cigarette out on the sole of his black combat boot, Drew glanced from Bell to Nicole and then back again. Both detectives' faces were devoid of any friendliness. His eyes blinked rapidly, and he swallowed convulsively. "Mandy and me were at a party."

"Now we're getting somewhere," Bell said, folding his arms across his chest. "Where was the party? Who saw you there? We'll need names and addresses, as well as names and addresses of the friends who were with you when you harassed Kevin Myers at the restaurant."

"I-"

"I'd do as my partner suggests, Mr. Nichols," Nicole said quietly. "If you're innocent, there's nothing to worry about."

Drew chewed his lower lip, frowning. Finally, he grudgingly rattled off a number of names and addresses, which Nicole copied down.

Bell then set about seeing what else he could find out about the loser sitting in front of him. "Where do you work, Drew?"

The younger man shrugged. "I'm kind of in between jobs right now. They're hard to come by - you know, with the economy tanking and all."

"Yeah, especially if you don't exactly try very hard to find one and spend all your time partying and harassing people. How about Mandy? She have a job?"

"She waitresses at a bar a couple nights a week. What's it to you?"

Bell looked around. "Do you own or rent?"

"We're looking after it for my grandma. She's in a home."

"You're not doing such a hot job, are you? I doubt Grandma would be too thrilled with your housekeeping skills." With his foot, Bell nudged a Chinese takeout carton that still had some rice stuck to the inside.

Drew had the grace to flush at that, but he didn't reply.

"And how about this?" He swooped down and grabbed the Stormfront pamphlet. "Are you a member?"

"So what if I am? It's a free country."

Bell began reading aloud. "'Your children's heritage is being stolen from them, right under your noses, and handed over to strangers, to those who hate them, who hate you, who despise European civilization and everything it stands for. We know who works to destroy us as a race and as a nation and we know why. And we know the saddest truth of all: They are succeeding.' Do you really believe this crap? That you're one of the 'keepers of the light?'"

Shifting in his seat, Drew just grinned.

"I see here that there's an online dating service for 'heterosexual white Gentiles only.' Was that how you met Mandy?"

Drew stood up. "Look, it's none of your fucking business what I do in my spare time. It's all legal." He pushed his way past them toward the door, which he held open. "I've told you what you want to know. Go ahead and talk to my friends. They'll tell you what I did and where I was. They'll tell you I was at a party Friday and didn't have nothin' to do with offing no clumsy nigger."

Shrugging, Bell accepted the invitation to leave, followed by Nicole. "No problem. We're done here anyway. Be sure to stick around. I'm sure we'll have more questions for you eventually."

The door slammed behind them.

"What a little shit." Nicole's vernacular was unusually crass.

"What did I just hear you say?"

"Honestly, people like that are enough to make a nun swear. Where does he get off acting like that?"

"He probably thinks life handed him a raw deal, so he's entitled to get something back — like we all owe him something and he doesn't have to do a thing for it."

Nicole snorted derisively. "Plenty of people get raw deals in life. It's not necessarily the end of the world." She knew first hand.

"Well, you and I know that, but unfortunately, people like Drew Nichols and his girlfriend haven't a clue."

"By the way, John, you crossed a line in there. You may want to ease up with the bad cop bit," Nicole said.

"You're overreacting. I barely touched the guy," Bell replied.

"I'm just saying, you need to control your temper, especially around the toads," Nicole explained.

He sighed. "Let's head back to the Roundhouse."

Drew waited for Bell and Nicole to drive off, then took the stairs two at a time to the bedroom he and Mandy shared. It wasn't his grandmother's room; for some reason, he couldn't bring himself to defile that space, and it was quite like she'd left it when she'd left to be admitted to the nursing home. He paused at her threshold, looking at the bed covered with a faded floral comforter and the dusty dresser covered with perfume bottles and pictures of family. Tears stung at the back of his eyes, which made him angry rather than introspective. He quickly averted his gaze from the tranquil scene and with a few short steps, he was in the other room.

The difference between the two rooms was stark. One was bright and clean in spite of the dust; the other smelled of marijuana and stale sex. He looked at Mandy, who was sitting on a beanbag that had lost most of its little Styrofoam balls, and getting ready to toke up. She was looking at him in a way he didn't like, so he took a step toward her, his hand balled into a fist. "What the hell is your problem?" He was pleased to see her shrink back a little.

"What did they want?" she asked.

"They think I offed some nigger," he barked out a short laugh.

"Well?"

"Well what?"

"Did you?"

"If I did, do you think I'd tell you? Last thing I need is for you to crack under pressure and squeal like that stupid old cow next door."

"You think she had something to do with them coming over today?"

"I wouldn't put it past the old bat. She'd better not do anything else to piss me off." He pressed his lips firmly together. His grandmother's old friend was a little too nosy for his liking.

Mandy finally got the joint lit and inhaled deeply, then handed it off to Drew. "Did you think she was hot?"

Drew's face registered confusion. "Who? The old bat?"

Mandy rolled her eyes. "That lady cop. I saw the way you looked at her."

Drew hated it when she pouted.

"So what if I looked at her? Lookin's free, ain't it?" He drew deeply on the joint, holding the smoke in his lungs as long as he could. He then placed it in a cheap orange plastic ashtray on the floor and took a step toward Mandy. Leaning down, he pushed her into a prone position and straddled her. She wiggled provocatively.

"Now?"

Drew thought about the blonde detective, and his pulse began racing. Even though she was younger than Nicole by about ten years, Mandy was nowhere near as attractive. In fact, she was kind of scrawny. But she was there and willing. He fumbled with the snap on her jeans and yanked them down, then pushed her shirt up so he could see her breasts; she never wore a bra.

His breathing quickened.

"Now."

Chapter Six

When they made it back to HQ, Sergeant Baker was waiting, and he was in a foul temper. "Well, well. I see Tweedle Dee and Tweedle Dum managed to make it back."

"We were questioning suspects, sir," Bell spoke through gritted teeth.

"Anything substantial?"

"Nothing to go on yet. We're still gathering information, and we've still have a lot of ground to cover."

"Make it snappy. That nosy bitch from *The Inquirer* keeps calling. Seems our friends at Blaq Unity have given her a hot tip that this crime may have been racially motivated."

Bell swore under his breath.

"What was that?" Baker snapped.

"How would you like us to handle it, sir?"

"You don't need to handle anything. Leave it to the captain and me. Just keep your noses to the ground and let me know the second you find anything." And with that, he stomped into to his office.

Bell had mixed feelings about activist groups. There were some, like the ones that existed to support members of the military or raised funds for serious diseases, which served a very worthwhile purpose. Then there were others that seemed to exist only to stir up the pot by grievance mongering. In his mind, Blaq Unity was of the latter type. For example, rather than address problems such as poor educational opportunities, absentee fathers, and dependence upon government handouts in the inner cities, they pointed their collective fingers at the police and any other government agency that they felt didn't cater enough to their numerous demands. Every time a black person was the victim of a crime, there they were, accusing the police of racism if someone wasn't arrested right away. By the same token, when a black person was accused of a crime, they often accused the police of racism for daring to charge him or her, even if there were over a dozen witnesses and video footage.

The nation had come a long way from institutional racism, but Bell felt he was being realistic in assuming it would never be swept away entirely. And anyone, regardless of their color or creed, could be guilty of it; he saw it in practice each and every day. But Bell saw racism not as an inherent societal condition, since society as a whole, had evolved quite a bit; rather, he saw it as a human condition that could not be legislated away, although certain politicians certainly thought it was possible. Thus they created "official" victim groups and furthered the Balkanization of American society (and their reelection prospects by fostering class envy and promising all things to all people).

Bell could see that Blaq Unity might prove to be a sizeable thorn in his side during the Myers case, and he hoped Sergeant Baker and the captain would continue to run interference so he and Nicole could concentrate on getting the job done.

Mid-morning Monday, the two detectives were no closer to an answer than they had been in the very wee hours of Saturday morning when they'd first gone to the crime scene. Between Bell, Nicole, and Detectives Brian Karpinsky and Bill King, they had contacted all the people Drew Nichols had provided as alibis. A few of them had remembered him being at the party with Mandy, while a few of them were fuzzy on the details, probably too hammered at the time to remember much of anything.

They had also spoken to the two guys who had been with Drew at Durkin's when the dust-up between Drew and Kevin occurred. Bell came across all sorts of undesirable characters in his work, and Drew's pals were no exception. The irony, of course, was that while they ranted and raved at an unjust world that had given them the shaft, they were still at home, living in their parents' basements. *Let them get a job,* Bell thought, *and see how much time they have for whining and complaining. And what's with the parents who put up with them?* He could only come to the conclusion that there were some mysteries in the world that would never be solved.

So while Drew's involvement in Kevin's murder could not be proven, he wasn't completely absolved either. As a precaution, Bell had asked that a couple of uniforms keep an eye on his activities while they were cruising the neighborhood.

While Nicole was up to her eyeballs in paperwork and phone calls, Bell was on his way to the Crime Scene Unit to talk to Simon Cleary.

Bell had never been a big fan of science. When he was in high school, he had often referred to the loathsome subject as "that boring hour after history and before lunch." Bell had always been a gifted student, but science was his academic Kryptonite, so, when he was forced to make his regular trip to the department's Forensic Sciences Division – otherwise known as the Crime Lab – the detective was less than enthused.

Bell appreciated the work of the Forensics people, and showed them the utmost respect, but a day spent getting his back waxed seemed preferable by comparison.

After pulling into the expansive parking lot, Bell stepped out of his unmarked sedan and made his way to the double doors at the front of the unit. The fairly new building, only a few years old, was a large three-story structure with a brick façade that occupied half a city block. The building housed the Crime Scene Unit, the Chemical Laboratory, the DNA Laboratory, and the Firearms Identification Unit – one-stop shopping for all your criminal investigatory needs.

Bell passed through the double doors and approached the security room. Most of the officers who worked the desk were old-timers riding out their last days before retirement, but they were still sharp as a tack when it came to spotting intruders who didn't work there and had no business entering the facility. Luckily for Bell, most of the officers knew him by sight, and entering the building was a snap - usually. Not today.

A short, heavyset woman was manning the security desk, and she gave Bell an unwelcome look. Nevertheless, Bell tried to make nice.

"Good morning. I'm Detective Bell from Homicide, here to see Simon Cleary."

The female officer rolled her eyes. "Do you have your ID?"

"Sure," Bell said. "Here is my badge."

The officer was unimpressed. "Sir, I need to see your badge *and* your Police ID. Surely you know that."

This was the point where Nicole would have tried to calm Bell down and beg him not to pull the officer through the window, but Nicole wasn't with him.

"Yes, Officer, I do know that," he began. "I also know that your bright pink nail polish is in blatant violation of Directive 78, the department uniform code. I have my badge and ID with me. Do you have nail polish remover with you?"

The officer was beaten, and she knew it, but at least she didn't hold a grudge. "Go right on in, Detective," she said with a smirk.

As Bell walked down the hallway to Cleary's office, he couldn't help but notice the cleanliness of the new building. Most of the units used to be located at Police Headquarters. The CSU had been in an unbelievably dirty rat hole on the first floor, and most visitors wondered how any crimes were solved there. One jovial young detective had once remarked that Amelia

Earhart, Sasquatch, and Pamela Anderson's virginity were somewhere beneath all of that room's clutter. The new division was filet mignon to the old place's chopped liver. Bright, well-lit rooms with clean tile floors complemented sturdy, unblemished walls and comfortable workstations. Furnishings were modern and well kept, from functional desks and chairs to file cabinets and storage closets.

Civilian employees walked through the building wearing white lab coats and professional attire, while CSU officers dressed in blue polo shirts and blue work pants. Some of the CSU crew carried their service pistols with them, but many left them in the unit safe. In that place especially, there was no room for accidents. Almost all of the evidence that was submitted there belonged to high-profile felony cases such as homicides, rapes, and robberies. The fates of those cases – and the victims involved – rested within those pristine walls. Nobody entered the unit without clearance or supervision, an axiom that no one ever questioned.

Bell knocked before entering and was waved in by Simon Cleary, whose blond hair was as disheveled as usual. Sitting down in a cheap black chair across from Cleary's desk, Bell jumped right into it.

"Any developments in the Myers case?"

Cleary sighed, nodding toward a file folder on his desk. "From the apartment itself, nothing unusual has cropped up. We found a few sets of fingerprints that don't match Myers's, but none of them were a match for anything in our database. They could belong to anyone, like his landlord or his friends. No blood, no bodily fluids, nothing out of the ordinary. Now, in the trunk of the Sebring, we did find fibers that matched the clothing Myers was wearing when he was found, as well as hairs that matched Myers's hair, which indicates he was taken to the scene from another location. Unless something else magically crops up, though, I don't think we can say 100 percent that that location was his apartment. Oh, and speaking of hair, we did find a few that didn't match his, nor do they match the sample we obtained from the car owner."

"Well, it's something."

"Yes, it's possible that those hairs could be used to help identify the doer down the line. We still have to do some testing, but they were of medium length, black, and fairly smooth. Oh, and something else…"

"Go on."

"When examining his clothing, we discovered a bit of ground-in motor oil on his shirt."

"Motor oil?"

"Yes, on the front."

"Hmm." Bell's mind was going over the possibilities. "Perhaps there was oil on the ground where he was attacked, and it got on the shirt during the struggle."

"That's plausible."

Bell rose. "Thanks, Simon. Keep us posted of any new developments."

Cleary nodded. "We'll be in touch."

As he headed back to Homicide, Bell continued to mull over this latest development – or non-development, however one chose to look at it. Kevin Myers very likely hadn't been killed at home. If their suspicions were correct and the oil on his shirt indicated that he'd been attacked either in an alleyway, parking lot, or street, that meant he could have bought it just about anywhere. Also, he'd told Emma he planned to stay in Friday night, snacking and watching television. *So why did he go out? Just taking a walk to get some fresh air, to stretch his legs? Did he decide to run to a nearby convenience store to pick up something to go with his chips and salsa? Or did someone stop by and convince him to go out instead of relaxing on the couch?*

Whatever the reason, Kevin Myers was now dead, and it just didn't make much sense, as far as Bell could figure. He was a quiet guy with no known enemies, living a quiet life, and he ended up having his life snuffed out unexpectedly. In his own mind, Drew Nichols seemed the most likely suspect, but there just wasn't enough proof of it. *Not yet.*

When he got back to Homicide, Bell found a desk near where Nicole was sitting and tossed his light jacket on the back of the chair and plopped down. Nicole was just finishing up a phone call, so Bell sat waiting, jiggling his leg up and down, a nervous habit he'd inherited from his father. She turned to him as she hung up, wearing a smile on her face.

"Well? Don't keep me in suspense."

Nicole reached up to readjust her high blonde ponytail as she spoke. "I finally talked to the local Army recruiter. He was able to track down Kevin Myers's unit and his commanding officer, a Captain James McBride. Kevin enlisted right out of high school. He did a tour in Afghanistan and was honorably discharged about a year ago when his contract was up. He didn't reup."

Bell whistled. "The 'Stan?"

"Yep. I just put in a call to the number the recruiter gave me, and they promised to get my message to Captain McBride and have him call me as soon as he can. He's still overseas, so I gave them my cell phone number and told them he could call me anytime, day or night."

"Any idea what his specialty was?" Bell asked, aware that in the modern Army, recruits usually specialize in one area.

Nicole consulted her notes. "Yeah...an MLRS repairer."

Bell cocked an eyebrow.

"Multiple launch rocket system," she clarified.

"What the hell do they do?"

"Maintenance, troubleshooting - a lot of technical know-how about electronics and mechanics."

"Gee. You'd think he'd be able to find a better job than working in some crappy restaurant. Maybe he could have apprenticed with an electrician or become a mechanic or something."

"You'd think," Nicole concurred, "but look at this." She pointed to an article she'd found online. "I was on hold for a few minutes, and I found this while waiting. It says here that official unemployment figures for recent vets were twice that of civilians, and nearly 20 percent of soldiers just back from tours of duty were out of work. Of those who found jobs, about a quarter of them pay less than $22,000 a year. Apparently, HR directors don't see veterans as seasoned professionals who can be counted on when things get tough. They see them as 'damaged goods.'" She snorted. "They volunteer to protect their country, put their lives on the line, and what do they get? Thanks but no thanks. What a load of crap."

Bell nodded in agreement. He'd briefly considered joining the military at one time, but an incident in his younger days was quick to steer him down a different path. When he was a sophomore in high school, he was walking home from a dance with a friend when they were jumped by the local white trash. They knocked Bell and his friend down, kicked the living hell out of them, and took their money. Bell knew who they were, but he wrote it off. Back then, no one called the police for anything, so he didn't see the point. It was that night, though, as he walked home nursing his arm and bloody face, he swore he was going to go into law enforcement.

When he got to college, he was considering taking a job with the Feds, but in early 1990s the economy sucked, so he took the first job that was offered: the PPD. He figured only be there until the Feds called, but eleven years later, he was a detective, with a lot of prestige within the department and a decent salary to match – even though he often thought they weren't paying him enough for some of the crap he had to put up with. He often told himself, *I am a detective in one of the largest police departments in the country. That has to count for something.* Still, he maintained a healthy dose of respect for the military, and it steamed him to think that veterans weren't being hired because they were seen as "damaged goods." *Nice homecoming.*

Nicole broke in on his thoughts, as she often seemed to do. "What next?"

Scratching his ear for a moment, Bell considered their options. "How about heading back down to our favorite restaurant? We still need to talk to some of the other employees."

"Okay. Let me just freshen up a bit." Nicole rose to head to the ladies' room. As she passed through the room, she could feel covert glances coming from a few of her fellow detectives. As one of the few women in the Homicide Division – and one of the most attractive ones at that – she was often on the receiving end of sexism, both concealed and blatant. It bothered her at times, but she knew if she kicked up a stink every time she saw a girlie calendar or heard a racy joke or a colleague checked her out, she'd be persona non grata. The police were a tight bunch. So long as she didn't whine, she earned a grudging amount of respect. Nicole knew some of her female colleagues were talked about behind their backs for being snitches because they were constantly harping on every little thing, but it was her opinion that women joining the force should know it's a man's world, and it isn't going to change overnight; she accepted that fact with as much grace as she could muster, and her co-workers respected her for that.

Her mother hadn't been pleased with her career choice any more than Bell's was with his. She wondered why her daughter couldn't have chosen to be a teacher, or an accountant, or a lawyer, or some other professional job where she could work 9:00 to 5:00, have weekends off, and work her way up the corporate ladder to the fabled corner office and six-figure salary. Nicole knew what bothered her mother the most was the danger she faced on a daily basis, although some of that fear had abated once she was out of uniform and no longer patrolling the streets. But her mother also knew Nicole well enough to know that constantly voicing her fears would get her nowhere, so she kept her admonitions to a simple "Be careful" whenever winding up a conversation on the phone.

Nicole knew her husband, Jeff Ellis, didn't worry nearly as much as his mother-in-law. After all, as a man, he was quite capable of understanding and appreciating the adrenaline rush associated with dangerous occupations, even though he himself was a suit, a corporate lawyer. Even still, he enjoyed sports like rock-climbing and mountain biking. These were some of the things that the two of them enjoyed together, although lately Nicole had him working on projects around the house. In her mid-thirties, she had begun to feel the urge to "nest." Jeff wanted children too, but he had to wonder, *Are we ready for the one that's on the way?*

When they entered Durkin's, it was reminiscent of their first visit, in that there wasn't much activity during the lull between breakfast and lunch. A few customers lingered over coffee, but the place was relatively empty, and Bell and Nicole noted a few waitresses huddled behind the counter in deep conversation. When the door opened, both detectives looked up and saw a familiar face.

Emma Watson recognized the detectives immediately. She flushed slightly, tucked a few hairs that were escaping from her ponytail behind her ear, and smoothed her apron. She smiled as Bell and Nicole approached her, but her smile reminded Bell of the wistful face of Vermeer's *"Girl with a Pearl Earring"* a painting he'd seen in a book when he took an art history course back in college. She spoke first.

"Have you found anything out yet? Do you know who did it?"

"Unfortunately, no, but we're pursuing several leads."

Emma sighed, then turned to her co-workers. "I remember you wanted to talk to Lori, Wanda, and Heather. This is Lori, and this is Heather. Wanda will be in later."

Bell and Nicole exchanged greetings with the waitresses, and then Bell turned back to Emma. "Is your boss in?"

"No. He's not scheduled to come in until later. Brandi opened today, and she'll be here until about three."

"Where can I find her?"

"I think she's in the office. I'll show you the way."

Bell whispered to Nicole, and she nodded, turning to Lori and Heather as Bell followed Emma toward a door.

Emma knocked on the door, even though it was slightly ajar. "Brandi? Brandi, one of the detectives is here to talk to you."

Her knock caused the door opened to reveal a room that was more like a closet. Tucked behind the restrooms, it barely had enough space for the old metal desk covered with receipts, vendor invoices, and other office debris. Hunched over an adding machine was Brandi, who turned to look at the visitors. Bell guesstimated her to be somewhere in her late twenties. Her dark, bobbed hair was held back from her forehead with a pink headband, and a pale sprinkling of freckles dotted her cheekbones. She pushed her work aside. "Won't you come in?" She indicated a straight-backed wooden chair that was crammed in a corner next to the desk.

Bell squeezed himself in, smiling his thanks to a blushing Emma as she excused herself. "I'm Detective Bell." He held out his hand.

"Brandi Davis."

They shook briefly.

"My partner, Detective Ellis, is speaking to a couple of waitresses out front. We're investigating the murder of Kevin Myers."

Brandi's eyes misted briefly. "I know. Everyone liked Kevin. We're all still in shock."

"That's what I keep hearing."

"What?"

"That everyone liked Kevin. Well, someone must not have liked him for one reason or another."

"I can't think of anyone here who felt that way about him. He was just a really sweet guy." Her hands were clenched together. "So, what can I help you with?"

"Just a few routine questions."

"Okay."

"I understand you weren't here that night."

She nodded. "It was my night off. I went out to the movies with a girlfriend, then we went for a couple of drinks."

"See anything good?"

"Not really – just some stupid comedy that'll be on DVD in a month or two. A real waste of money, if you ask me. Still, it was nice to get out and do something besides work."

"I take it your friend will be able to vouch for you?"

Brandi's eyebrows came together slightly. "Of course."

"Could I have her name and a contact number?" He pulled a small notebook out of his pocket.

"You don't think…God, you don't think that maybe I-"

"I don't know what to think, Miss Davis. Right now we need to gather as much information as possible, and part of that is finding out where everyone with any kind of connection to Kevin was on the night of his murder. So, if you don't mind?" She gave him a name, Jennifer Morris, and a number, which he jotted down in what his teachers had always described as his chicken scratch. "Oh, and can you spell your name for me?"

"Brandi, with an i."

Bell almost laughed. It sounded like one of those made-up names of B-list actresses, like Barbi Benton back in the 1970s, whom he remembered from her guest stints on *"The Love Boat"* and *"Fantasy Island"* more than he did for having been Hugh Hefner's girlfriend. He quickly brought himself back to the present.

"Thanks. What about someone at home?"

"What do you mean?"

"Do you live with anyone? Someone who can vouch for when you got back from your night out on the town?"

"Oh." Brandi seemed surprised. "Yeah, I share an apartment with my cousin Chrystal. Chrystal Brewster."

"You get along with Chrystal?"

"Yeah, we get along okay…well, enough to be roommates."

"Now," Bell continued, "what can you tell me about Kevin? His friends? Do you know anything that might give us some answers."

She shrugged. "He was really quiet, you know? Didn't do much socializing that I know of." Bell nodded; he'd heard this already.

"I've been told he was kind of palling around with a couple guys who work in the kitchen."

"Yeah, Lawrence Jenkins and Daryl Davis. I don't know much, but they did things together once in a while – you know, movies, maybe play some basketball, whatever guys do, I guess."

"Mm hmm. Are they in today? I'd like to talk to them after we're through here."

Brandi nodded. "Sure, no problem."

"I heard a rumor that your boss doesn't always follow the rules about who he hires and that he pays guys under the table. Know anything about that?"

"No, and if I did, I'd be a fool not to report him."

Bell nodded and moved on. "How about Mr. Durkin? How did Kevin get along with him?"

Again, she shrugged. "Just like the rest of us, I suppose. He can be kind of a hard-ass at times, but he's no worse than anyone else I've worked for. Kevin did tell me once that he was really grateful to Durkin for hiring him. He'd gotten out of the Army and was having a hard time finding a job." Bell thought back to the newspaper article he'd seen on line earlier that morning about veterans being shunned by the private work sector. *Wait…If he was grateful, would he have done anything for his benefactor? Perhaps even something illegal that might have gotten him into trouble?* He posed this question to Brandi.

"Like the mafia?" She barked out a laugh. "Durkin runs the business okay, but that's about it. And I don't see him having the time - or, frankly – the brains to do much else."

"That's no way to talk about your boss." But Bell smiled, thinking of Sergeant Baker back at headquarters.

Brandi smiled back. She had a pleasant smile, and she seemed more relaxed than she have during the beginning of the interview. Bell marked it off as the usual jitters people have when being questioned by police, even if they haven't done anything wrong, similar to the rush of adrenaline most people experience when being pulled over on the road.

"So you can't think of anything or anyone that could have had anything to do with Kevin being murdered? What about the incident a few weeks ago, when he got into a scrap with some customers?"

Brandi rolled her eyes. "I wasn't here for that, fortunately, but I heard about it. A real couple of losers, I guess, but there was more bark than bite, I imagine. I heard they took off pretty fast when Durkin threatened to call the police."

"But maybe they were mad enough to get their revenge on him later."

"Maybe. I don't know."

Bell stood up. Feeling a bit cramped, he rubbed the back of his neck with his hand. "Thanks for your time. Here's my card. If you can think of anything else, please don't hesitate to call. I'd like to talk to Daryl and Lawrence now, if it's not too much trouble," he reminded her.

"Yeah, I'll get them for you. You might as well stay here. I know it's crowded, but at least it's private. The kitchen can get kind of noisy."

"Actually, give me a minute. I'll be right back." He dashed out to the dining room, where Nicole was still talking to the waitresses. He called her aside. "Are you done with them?"

"Pretty much. Why?"

"The two guys Kevin was friends with, Lawrence and Daryl, are here, and I want to interview them, but not together. Will you take one and I can take the other?"

Nicole opened her mouth to reply, but her cell phone began ringing. She pulled it out of her pocket.

"Ellis. Yes. Oh yes, hold on." She placed her hand over the mouthpiece. "It's Myers's commanding officer. I have to take this call." She pointed to the car and started out the door. Bell went back to the office, where Brandi was waiting with a confused look on her face.

"Sorry about that. I had to talk to Detective Ellis about something. Could you bring the guys in now?"

"Sure."

As Brandi headed to the kitchen, Bell thought about how he'd handle the questioning. Even though they weren't necessarily suspects, he'd wanted Nicole to talk to one and him the other, just in case something was fishy. He could have asked for one at a time, but he knew time was short because the lunch crowd would be in soon, and they would both probably be too busy. He decided he'd have to make the best of it; he was nothing if not adaptable.

Moments later, the three of them were crowded into the small office. Daryl was slightly taller and heavier than Lawrence and had a darker complexion. His head was shaved, while Lawrence sported corn rows. Both men looked slightly apprehensive, so Bell did his best to put them at ease.

"Hi. I'm Detective Bell. I'm here to talk about Kevin." The two men nodded. "Can you tell me about your relationship with him? You were friends, right?"

"Yeah, I guess," Daryl said.

"Did you do things together? Spend time together?"

"Mostly just talk, maybe watch TV in Kevin's apartment. You know, we just sorta hung out."

"Ah, okay. Where were you last Friday night?"

"Last Friday night?" Daryl echoed.

"Yes, the night Kevin was killed."

"We were off that night. We were at a party."

"A party? Where?"

"My cousin's house," Daryl said.

"Were you there all night?"

"Pretty much."

"And the other people at the party would remember you being there?" The two men nodded.

Bell changed his tack quickly, quite on purpose. "How long have you been working here?"

"Me? Two years," Daryl replied. "Lawrence's been here for -"

"I'd like to hear it from Lawrence, if you don't mind." Bell was reminded of the comic magician duo Penn and Teller, where Penn did all the talking.

"Well, Lawrence? How long have you been working here?"

"Two years."

"So you both started working here about the same time? You were working here when Kevin started?"

"Yes." Again, Daryl answered for both of them.

Bell asked them a few more questions about Kevin, but like everyone else, they seemed to know little, despite having "hung out" with him. Bell noticed that both men seemed twitchy and nervous about something. *But what?* He wondered about the anonymous tip he'd received and whether there was any truth to it, despite Brandi's avowal of the opposite.

"If you remember anything, please give us a call. And I'll need to know how to reach Daryl's cousin to check your alibi. Can you give me a name and phone number?"

Daryl said his cousin's name was Tyrone Davis and gave an address in Frankford, along with a phone number.

After the two men had returned to the kitchen, Bell said goodbye to Brandi and Emma, telling them that he and Nicole would be in touch soon, and went back out to the sedan where Nicole was just clicking off her cell phone. He hopped in the driver's seat and waited expectantly.

"Captain McBride had some very interesting information about our Kevin." Nicole related that McBride had had little to complain about as far as Kevin's ability as a soldier. He was friendly (*there's that word again*), adapted fairly quickly to military life, and got along well with his fellow troops.

"Apparently, though," she said, "he was a bit on the innocent side."

"What does that mean?"

"Gullible, easily fooled. He was somewhat naïve, and that made him the butt of a lot of practical jokes - you know, the kind of pranks people in close quarters love to play on each other."

"How did he take that?"

"From what Captain McBride said, he had a pretty good attitude about it all. Everyone seemed to like him. It wasn't until he got news of his parents' death that he seemed to change. He got depressed, of course. He received an early discharge because of it, although he only got out a couple of months earlier than he might have otherwise."

"What about combat? Did he see any action over there?"

"Captain McBride couldn't be too specific due to military hush orders, but theirs was a support unit, not a combat one. From what I could gather, they were involved in a skirmish or two."

"So there's the possibility of post-traumatic stress disorder? PTSD syndrome?"

"Maybe. I suppose we could find out if he's received any counseling services from the VA."

Bell shook his head. "I don't know how necessary that is at this point, but it's something we can look into later if need be. What about the ladies at the diner? One of them was Wanda, right?"

"Yes, Wanda and Lori. What a couple of gossip hounds! I feel like I know all the dirt about everyone at that place, and I only talked to them for a few minutes."

Bell knew the type. He'd dated a few over the years, and they usually wore on him quickly. He had to snoop into people's lives as a part of his job – often discovering enough dirty laundry in one case to fill an entire supermarket tabloid. Unfortunately, the kind of gossip he uncovered was connected to gruesome murders. So spending his free time prying into others' personal lives didn't have the same appeal as it did for some people.

"Well? Don't you want to know what I found out?"

"Shoot."

"You know the assistant manager, Brandi?"

"What about her? She had an attitude at first, but that's not unusual. She ended up being pretty helpful."

"Considering what I heard, I wouldn't be surprised if you told me she seemed a bit antagonistic. Seems she had the hots for Kevin, but he didn't return the favor."

"Really?" That put things in a brand new light. "A spurned lover?"

"I don't think it even got that far. It was pretty obvious that she liked him, and she apparently asked him out a couple of times, but he always turned her down." Nicole glanced at her notebook. "I guess things were a bit frosty on Brandi's end after that."

"Hmm." Bell's mind was racing. "Could she have had a couple of friends beat him up to teach him a lesson and things got out of hand?"

"Or maybe some of her friends found out she was interested in a black guy and didn't like it?" They looked at each other.

"She didn't admit to knowing the charming Drew, but who knows? I guess I'll have to have another chat with her, and soon." Bell frowned. "Did you find out anything else that might be interesting?"

"Only that Durkin is some kind of perv."

"What do you mean by that? Does he hit on the help? Customers?"

"No, but apparently he spends a lot of time at Dalia's Delights. Didn't he say he took Kevin there for his birthday?"

"Yeah, and we still haven't had a chance to head over there to check it out. I'll see if Karpinsky and King can stop by later today or tomorrow. Probably not much to it – just an older guy who likes to get his rocks off."

It wasn't illegal, but Bell thought men who frequented strip clubs on a regular basis were a bit creepy, especially the ones who were old enough to be the strippers' grandfathers. Bell grimaced when he thought of the current fitness craze among middle-class women, learning how to pole dance. Even worse was that such classes were even being offered to children. What might be "empowering" at a gym or in a nice suburban living room was far from the reality of the seedy world of "gentlemen's entertainment." Many of the women were engaged in nonstop drinking and drugs. They spent their money as fast as they earned it and partied hard with the men they met. Too many of them ended up dead, either from an overdose or by more sinister means, and Bell had seen more of his share of such sad cases. Those who didn't die usually ended up bitter and aged before their time.

"So what about the kitchen help?" Nicole asked.

"Nothing jumped out at me, but we'll keep an eye on them just in case." Bell shrugged. He checked the time on his phone and saw it was nearly lunchtime. They decided to grab a bite and then continue on from there.

Just as they were finishing lunch at a local burger stand, Nicole's cell phone buzzed. Bell waited as she took the call, and she turned to him as she clicked the phone off. "Kevin Myers's aunt and uncle have arrived. They're down at HQ."

Bell sighed heavily. It was time to talk to the grieving family and dig around to find out anything that could possibly shed light on the murder without offending anyone. "Okay, let's go."

Chapter Seven

Leon and Norma Myers sat across from the two detectives in a small, dreary interview room.

Interview rooms are not designed to be conducive to friendly, comfortable chats. The cinderblock walls are painted a light puke green, and there is only one place available to sit – a flat, non descript table in the center of the room. There is a chair for the defendant/suspect on one side of the table, bolted into the floor. The chair has a set of handcuffs, with one cuff locked to the chair, where a suspect's weak arm would be fastened so his or her strong hand would be free to sign off on the Miranda rights, confessions, or whatever else needed his or her John of Jane Hancock. There are two other chairs on the opposite side for the detectives. Defendants are always interviewed with just two detectives: one on the lead, one as backup.

Leon Myers was sitting in the suspect's chair, and another chair had been brought in for his wife. The couple looked to be close to sixty, Bell thought, and they looked tired from their long trip. Wearing casual clothing that was a bit rumpled from all the time they'd spent in the plane that day, neither of them seemed to be much interested in taking a sip of the coffee in front of them. After all, they had just been to the morgue.

Nicole spoke first. "I'm sorry about the room. This was the only place available."

"Can you tell us what happened?"

"That's what we're trying to figure out, Mr. Myers," said Bell. He told them as much as he could about Kevin's death without going into gory details or giving away information that might jeopardize the investigation. He doubted the distraught-looking couple had anything to do with it, but caution was always a priority. Norma Myers was trying to stay calm, but tears trickled down her cheeks. Her husband held her hand tightly with his own work-worn hand.

"Do you have any suspects?" she asked, wiping away a tear with a tissue from the box Nicole had thoughtfully placed there.

Bell leaned forward slightly. "We're working on a couple of leads. I assure you, Mrs. Myers, that we're doing everything possible to find the person who did this. It's still very early in the investigation."

"We're hoping you can tell us about Kevin. We've heard from his co-workers and also from his commanding officer in the Army. Background information can sometimes be very helpful," added Nicole.

Leon Myers pushed his untouched cup of coffee aside and leaned his elbows on the table. "What exactly do you want to know?"

"Anything about his friends, personality quirks, things like that."

"Well," Leon began slowly, "he's my younger brother's boy, their only son. Darrell and Judy doted on that boy. Kevin never gave them any trouble. The kid did okay in school and kept his nose clean."

"Did he grow up here in Philly?" Bell wondered.

"Darrell and Judy moved here in the late eighties, before Kevin started school, when Darrell was transferred up here."

"He was such a sweet little boy," Norma added. "We loved having him down to visit. He got along well with our children, and they always had a good time together."

"Where do your children live now, Mrs. Myers?" Nicole was jotting down everything the couple said.

"Bob lives in Atlanta with his wife and Aaron lives in Missouri." *That moat likely rules them out,* Nicole thought, *but we'll have to check anyway.*

Leon chuckled fondly. "Kevin was kind of a sucker though."

"A sucker?"

"It was always easy to fool him. Our boys liked to play jokes on him. Nothing mean-spirited, mind you, and it was all in good fun, the way cousins do. Kevin usually ended up laughing with everyone else at the end. He was also the kind of guy who would do anything for anybody. He'd give you the shirt off his back."

Nicole flashed Bell a quick look, recalling that Kevin's commanding officer had said something similar about him. If they were right and Brandi had been involved, it may have been quite simple for her to lure him to his fate. "Do you know why he decided to join the Army?"

"He didn't quite know what he wanted to do," Leon replied. "College didn't quite appeal to the boy, and he didn't have any interest in any particular trade, so he figured, why not the Army? He told us when he got home that he might go to college on the GI bill."

"Why didn't he?"

"I don't think he was quite ready for that." Norma's eyes filled with tears, but she managed to keep her voice steady. "He was devastated when his parents were killed in that car accident. He was almost done with his tour of duty when it happened, so the service discharged him early. After the funeral, he said he figured he'd find a job for a while, make some money, and then look into school."

One thing was bugging Bell. "Why didn't he go back to Georgia to be with family? Why come here, if there was no one left?"

Leon ran a hand over his eyes. "We tried to convince him to move down near us, but he said he felt as though Philadelphia was his home. Unfortunately, most of his friends had either moved from the area or were against the war and didn't want much to do with him when he got back. He kept in touch with us, mostly by phone – we talked about once a month – and he told us the owner of the restaurant…uh, Dobson, was it?"

"Durkin. Reginald Durkin."

"Right. Well Kevin told us this Durkin fellow had been good to him, giving him work when he couldn't find any and renting him the apartment. By the way, will we be able to meet him while we're here? I'd like to thank him for everything he did for our nephew."

"I'm sure there'll be an opportunity for that."

"Thank you." Leon hesitated briefly. "When can we…I mean, when will…" His voice trailed off.

"When can you claim the body?" Nicole gently finished his sentence.

"Yes. We'd like to take him back to Georgia. His parents were buried, and they have a family plot there."

"I'm afraid I can't say for sure," Bell said, "but I can't imagine it'll be more than a couple of days. The medical examiner's office is still waiting for some test results - standard stuff, but it's necessary, I'm afraid. Where are you staying? Do you have a hotel? If not, I can recommend a few that are reasonably priced."

Norma crumpled her tissue up and, not knowing where else to put it, tucked it into her purse. "We have some friends in the area. We'll be staying with them. Fortunately Leon had some vacation time saved up. His boss told him to take all the time he needs."

Bell handed them his card, and Nicole followed suit. "Is there a number where we can reach you? I promise we'll be in touch with all the latest developments."

Leon gave them his cell phone number, as well as the number of the friends with whom they were staying. Sensing the interview was over, the couple stood, and Nicole ushered them toward the door.

"Let me show you out."

Norma hesitated. "You will find out who did this, won't you?"

"I promise. We won't give up until the case is solved." As Nicole led them out, Bell indicated that he'd wait for her back in the detectives' room.

A few minutes later, he and Nicole were hashing over the case, and they spent a good half-hour going over their notes and observations. Bell argued that Drew Nichols troubled him. "He's the only viable suspect right now."

"But we don't have definitive proof at this point, just suspicion."

"Yes, but look at what we do have. Mandy, his girlfriend or whatever she is, is most likely a drug abuser. Remember her slurred speech and dilated pupils? We have enough probable cause to search the residence for narcotics and other contraband. Maybe that search will turn up more than we bargained for."

Even though Bell and Nicole were not assigned to the Narcotics Field Unit, probable cause would enable them to obtain a search warrant, and that in turn, would give them a chance to tear the house apart looking for drugs. If they just so happened to come across a weapon or some other incriminating evidence in their search, that would be gravy. In Bell's mind, Drew Nichols was a thug, and that meant he was also probably involved in other illicit activities.

Nicole finally agreed, and after deciding to request the warrant the next day the two exhausted detectives went to their respective homes for dinner and bed.

The new day greeted John Bell with a deafening thunderclap that jolted him out of his bed. It wasn't often that he slept so soundly, but when he did, an earthquake would have trouble stirring him. Renee used to joke that he could nap through a nuclear attack, and in the aftermath of World War III, only cockroaches and Bell would be left standing.

Cursing the weather gods, he stretched his arms, belted out a lengthy yawn, and opened the window shades. The skies were painted a foreboding battleship gray, and while the rain had not yet begun, it was certainly on the menu. The Myers case was giving him fits, but with any luck, the break he and Nicole so sorely needed would happen that very day, courtesy of a search warrant that they'd happily serve at Drew Nichols's Disston Street residence. After a quick shower and a bottle of Turkey Hill Diet Iced Tea (Bell rarely ate so early in the morning) he was in his car and on the way to police HQ.

While battling the rain and busy rush-hour traffic on Interstate 95, Bell replayed that day in his mind. The initial interview at Nichols's house did not yield much in the way of rock-solid evidence, but something about Drew did not seem right. Bell had a feeling that Nichols knew more than he was willing to say, and when they'd mentioned Myers's death, Nichols's eyes had betrayed him. Many in the Homicide Division knew that the legendary detective instincts were greatly exaggerated in prime-time TV, but it couldn't be completely ignored, either. In this case, Bell had to go with his instincts, and that began with preparing the search warrant for the Nichols place.

After parking his car at a nearby lot – Philadelphia police headquarters has less than 100 spaces for the hundreds of personnel assigned there – Bell realized that he'd forgotten his umbrella at home. Being the superstitious type, as he jogged the half-block to HQ, he fretted that it may be the omen of a very bad day. Upon entering the building, he offered a wave to Jimmy, the officer at the security desk, swiped his ID card, and made his way to the elevators. The notoriously slow elevator lived up to its reputation, taking a full minute to go from the lobby to the first floor. Muttering under his breath, Bell walked into Homicide, where he was greeted by Detective King.

"Morning, John! Is it raining out?" he asked, stating the obvious considering Bell's soggy appearance. "You know, they make these things called umbrellas these days."

"Get bent, Brian," Bell replied without missing a beat. Then the drippy detective settled into his desk, flipped through a few other active case files, and made his way to the search warrants, which were kept at the supervisor's desk. Bell signed out the next one - and inserted all of the pertinent information in the log. On his way back, he saw Nicole, who'd just walked in.

"Hey, nice of you to join us so bright and early," Bell teased.

"Get bent!" Nicole always loved getting Bell with his own line. "Are we ready for the search warrant?"

"Almost. You wanna type it for me?"

"Oh yeah, sure, Your Majesty," Nicole jested. "We both know that you're the king of search warrants, while I am the queen of arrest warrants. Get typing."

She was right, as Bell had a literary gift of gab that could impress most accomplished authors, and while he would not be writing the great American novel anytime soon, he knew he could wow the folks at the Bail Commissioner's Office with his vivid, descriptive search warrants. Thus, the typing began.

The first part of the form read as follows: "Identify items to be searched for and seized. (Be as specific as possible.)"

Bell typed in the following: "Narcotics, narcotics paraphernalia, and narcotics packaging, as well as any other physical evidence relating to the sale and distribution of narcotics from the listed residence. Include also proof of residence and any monetary profits from sale of the same."

The basic rule when obtaining a search warrant is that smaller is better. If a detective writes that he or she is looking for a large safe, for example, the search will be limited. There is no reason to look in a chest of drawers for a large safe, because, obviously, such a large item would not fit in the space provided. The helpful thing about narcotics (and narcotics packaging) is that they are usually very small, so the search can be very wide. Everything from a garage to a jewelry box can be searched and treated as suspect, and again, if other contraband is found during the search, that is recoverable as well.

Proof of residence is almost always included on a search warrant for a home. It is used to establish the difference between the owner and residents of the location and any persons who may be visiting the dwelling.

Bell completed the rest of the warrant and called the Bail Commissioner's Office at the Criminal Justice Center, five blocks away. After a short conversation, Bell turned to Nicole.

"We're good. The BC will be signing around noon."

"Okay." Nicole nodded. "You want me to round up some of the guys?"

"Nah. I know a few officers in the 15th District who can meet us out there - good cops who don't mind getting their hands dirty."

Located in the basement of Philadelphia's Criminal Justice Center (CJC), the Bail Commissioner's Office is always bustling with activity. The office is, in fact, a medium-sized courtroom, which includes the bail commissioner's bench, desks for aides and other judicial personnel, and a closed-circuit television setup. The room is separated by a floor-to-ceiling glass partition, with the courtroom on one side and a waiting area on the other. The waiting area is adorned with long benches set aside for police personnel, witnesses, and family members of arrestees.

Bell and Nicole entered the CJC and showed their badges to the sheriff so they could bypass the metal detectors. The duo walked straight for a few yards, then took the stairs down from the lobby, approached Room B-8, and entered.

"Oh, well isn't this just swell," Nicole said to Bell. "Packed house."

The rogue gallery turned their heads in unison, looked the detectives up and down, and went back to watching the proceedings.

"Damn. Do you think we could get away with calling the emergency judge and tell him we just don't feel like waiting?" Bell asked.

"Nice try, John," laughed Nicole.

On the rare case that a bail commissioner is not available, there is one "emergency judge" located in every division. The emergency judge can sign a search warrant at his residence, allowing the detectives to proceed. Unfortunately for Bell, no emergency judge in the city would sign a warrant just because a detective didn't want to wait in line. Bell approached the glass partition door and caught the bail commissioner's attention with a wave.

The commissioner's aide buzzed him in.

Judge Guillermo Rivera was in the middle of a bail hearing for a woman who'd been charged with heroin possession. Most hearings in Philadelphia are conducted via closed-circuit television, by which the defendant can see the judge and vice-versa. The defendant was a young, attractive girl with blonde hair. She had not yet suffered the "heroin face" that scarred most longtime users of the drug, but if Judge Rivera felt any sympathy for the girl, that eroded when he saw her home address.

"It says here that you live in Broomall. Is that correct?" Rivera asked.

"Yes, Your Honor," replied the girl.

"Well, I think I speak for most Philadelphians when I say we do not appreciate young, well-to-do suburbanites coming to our town to get a quick fix. And being that this is your second offense, I will not give you R.O.R. Bail is set at $5,000."

Nicole, who was listening to the hearing over the waiting room loudspeaker, stifled a giggle at the bail sentence. While the defendant is only forced to pay ten percent of the total amount, Judge Rivera made a pretty bold statement with his decision. It was nice when the system worked.

Finished with Suburban Girl, Judge Rivera welcomed Bell.

"Good afternoon, Detective. What do you have for me today?"

"Good afternoon, Your Honor," Bell began. "I have a search warrant for a property on Disston Street. We're looking for narcotics evidence."

After reading the search warrant, Rivera asked, "Do you swear or affirm that the information in this affidavit is correct to the best of your knowledge?"

Bell, holding up his right hand, replied, "Yes, Your Honor."

"Done," Judge Rivera said. He then signed the warrant and stamped it with the official judicial seal.

Bell and Nicole were in business. As the pair were leaving the courtroom, Bell flipped open his cell phone, and called his 15th District officers.

Officers Vince Reardon and Kate O'Donnell were not happy campers. On any normal day, they would have been working solo cars without partners. Today, their sergeant had sent them out on the emergency patrol wagon, to be tasked with answering radio calls and transporting prisoners - an assignment to which Reardon always responded, "This sucks." When Bell called them, they were en route to headquarters with another model citizen, a man who'd decided to use his wife as a punching bag.

Already annoyed, O'Donnell answered her cell phone.

"Hello?"

"Hey, cutie," Bell began. "You busy?"

"Hold on a second." Then, to their prisoner in the rear of the wagon, she screamed, "YO! SHUT THE HELL UP!" In a much sweeter voice, she got back on the phone.

"Hey, Johnny," she replied. "Right now, Reardon and I are transporting a toad to the cell room for 1511 car, but that shouldn't take too long. Do you need something?"

"Reardon?" Bell laughed. "How did you get stuck with that loser?"

"She has you on speaker phone, you jerk!" Reardon said.

Laughing again, Bell got to the point. "Nicole and I just got a search warrant for a house on Disston. We're headed up there now, and if you want to meet us, we can serve it together."

Copying down the Disston Street address, O'Donnell said, "Fantastic! Give us about a half-hour, and we'll meet you down the street."

Like most aggressive police officers, Reardon and O'Donnell craved action. They were usually the first to respond to priority calls and were good for a few arrests a week. Arrests were good, but court overtime was better, and serving a search warrant with Homicide almost always guaranteed court time down the road. Besides, Bell and Nicole always took care of them.

When the detectives pulled up to the Nichols residence, the rain was coming down in buckets. They opened the doors of the unmarked vehicle just as Reardon and O'Donnell pulled up in the 15th District wagon. The four exchanged pleasantries before walking up to the front door. Reardon loudly banged on the door with his nightstick.

After a moment, Drew Nichols appeared. Dressed in a dingy t-shirt and boxer shorts, he appeared much less coherent than he had been during their first meeting.

"Yeah?" Nichols said.

Nicole caught Nichols's eye and stated, "Drew Nichols, we have a search warrant for this residence. Open the door and step back. Now!"

Bell could tell his partner was really going to enjoy this.

"Cops again? Shit, you have got to be kidding me," Nichols mumbled. "Let me see this so-called warrant."

Nicole smiled. "Oh, don't worry, Johnny Cochrane. You'll see it. We'll even be nice and leave a copy of it here when we leave." She figured Nichols didn't realize that policy dictated that a copy of the warrant be left with the residents after service.

Officer Reardon volunteered to keep an eye on Drew, as he happened to be the only person in the house at the time. Guarding him was an easy task, considering the fool could hardly keep his eyes open and kept leaning way back in the chair. The idiot was obviously high, but nobody cared. With him temporarily out of commission, there was little risk that he'd try to interfere in their search.

Bell decided that he, Nicole, and Kate would begin the search on the second floor of the home and work their way down to the first. The trio ducked and dodged trash on their way up the dilapidated staircase, and each chose a bedroom to go through.

"Well, the good part is that if we trash the room looking for drugs, no one will notice," Kate remarked.

"Yeah," Bell agreed. "Be careful, Katie, and if you find something good, let everyone know."

"Will do."

Bell took the master bedroom, while Nicole and Kate took the spare bedrooms. They knew it was always a good idea to start in one area of a room and search in a pattern, whether clockwise, counterclockwise, or front to back. This way, there was less of a chance of something either being missed or checked over more than once. Bell liked to search left to right, and Nicole preferred back to front. Whatever worked was fine with them, and they knew what they were doing.

The master bedroom was located in the corner of the house. It was large and roomy, with windows on two walls and a high ceiling. The wallpaper on the walls looked decades old and was peeling at some of the corners - not that

Nichols would notice. The carpets were wall to wall, but there were heavy stains throughout and a large hole near the foot of the bed, almost as if a fire had been set there. Shaking his head, Bell decided he didn't want to know. Instead, he started searching the tall chest of drawers. The top drawer was filled with underwear and socks, and as distasteful as that sight was, Bell soldiered on, pulling items out and dropping them on the floor. The first drawer was clean of contraband.

The other three drawers were clean as well, as they contained t-shirts, shorts, jeans, and a few wrinkled dress shirts. *Apparently, Mr. Nichols is not a regular attendee of the Philadelphia Academy of Music.*

Bell moved on to the small chest of drawers and began another search. Unlike the police dramas boasted by the networks, no real detectives ever take out a drawer and dump the contents onto the floor. First, it would be a very sloppy way to search, and second, if there was contraband in there, such as a small amount of narcotics, it might get lost in the avalanche. For his part, Bell took out a clothing item, felt it, shook it around, and then dropped it. That method wasn't perfect and was somewhat time consuming, but it was fairly accurate. Five minutes later, Bell came up empty again, so he decided to move on to the bed.

The queen-sized bed seemed wasted in the room, since it was likely that Nichols just passed out wherever his heart – and the drugs – desired. The bed was connected to a wooden headboard that was equipped with a few small storage spaces, and a plain wooden footboard. Nichols was definitely a user, so Bell knew he might find drugs, but if Nichols did carelessly keep firearms in the house, the detective knew there was a good chance he'd keep a handgun near where he was supposed to sleep.

Opening the first small storage space, Bell saw something interesting. Try as he might, he just couldn't stifle his smile. There, just inches from the pillow, lay a Glock 21, .45-caliber, semiautomatic pistol. Bell picked the weapon up by the checkered grips – a good way to pick up firearms evidence since the grips rarely yield fingerprints - released the magazine catch, and locked the slide to the rear, ejecting a live round. The gun was loaded with thirteen rounds in the magazine and one in the chamber. The best part, though, from Bell's point of view, was the obliterated serial number on the frame. In many cases, such intentional damage would signify that the weapon was either stolen or previously used in a crime. What the criminals didn't know was an unreadable serial number only made it more difficult to trace the gun and its history – by no means impossible. Not only that, but possessing a firearm with an obliterated serial number is a felony, according to the Gun Control Act of 1968. It is a felony to file off a gun serial number and to sell or possess a gun with a filed serial number. Drew Nichols was about to have a very bad day.

Bell walked out of the master bedroom with his newfound booty and entered the room where Nicole was searching. She was bending down to look under the bed, and Bell found himself with a view he could only allow himself to think of as *"Interesting."*

"And me without my camera phone," Bell said.

Quickly turning her head, Nicole shot back, "You're going to be eating that phone in a second. Did you find anything?"

Holding up the Glock, Bell did his best Emeril Lagasse impersonation. "BAM!"

Nicole stood up, smiled from ear to ear, and asked, "Please tell me there is something more to this?"

"Give me 'Obliterated Serial Numbers' for $1,000!"

"Yes!" Nicole exclaimed.

"Can I go place the cuffs on this toad?" Nicole asked.

"Absolutely, as long as we name Reardon and O'Donnell as the arresting officers," Bell said.

"No problem," said Nicole. "I just want to see his face when I cuff his drug-addled ass."

Moments later, Officer O'Donnell also struck gold in the form of large baggie of marijuana and a few bundles (ten packets in each) of heroin. The stash of heroin was rather large to be considered "personal use," so the possession with intent to deliver (PWID) charge would be yet another felony for Nichols's ever-growing rap sheet.

The detectives informed Reardon and O'Donnell about the pistol before Nicole slapped the handcuffs on Drew Nichols. The officers escorted the man to the wagon, locked him in, and notified police radio that they were on their way to Homicide with one defendant. Nichols would be processed, fingerprinted, and have his mug shot taken in the Detention Unit before being taken upstairs to a grim and intimidating Homicide interrogation room, where Bell and Nicole would let him sit and worry until the drugs worked their way out of his system. Once he was sober enough to understand just how much trouble he was in, they'd read him his Miranda rights and have a real heart to heart.

Chapter Eight

While Drew Nichols was cooling his heels in a holding cell, Bell and Nicole split up. Nicole was headed back to Durkin's to question Brandi further, and Bell's destination was Dalia's Delights with Detective Karpinsky. Although Dalia's was considered a respectable place as far as strip joints went, Bell knew they employed muscle. Even though the reason for their visit was fairly benign, he was glad he brought Karpinsky along; there is always more safety in numbers. They arrived during a lull, between the lunchtime and after-work crowds.

Located on Passyunk Avenue, Dalia's was one of a number of gentlemen's and ladies' clubs in that area. It was housed in a non descript brick building with only a few boarded-over windows. While some clubs along that strip were quite upscale in their décor, menu, and the dancers themselves, Dalia's faded splendor competed with modern moral decay.

As typical for such an establishment, the interior was dark, with tables scattered throughout and a bar running along one wall. Doors opposite the bar led to small rooms where clients with means could be entertained privately. Despite the steady humming of the air filtration system, there was a lingering odor of stale cigarette and cigar smoke, mixed with something unrecognizable and unappealing. Waitresses wearing skimpy lingerie plied the few customers with drinks and food from the kitchen, while a woman clad only in a G-string gyrated on stage to the pulsating beat of generic music blaring from hidden speakers. Bell immediately noticed that all of the working girls were young, yet hardened, their tough visages were a result of seeing and experiencing more than they should have at any age.

Bell and Karpinsky approached the bar, where the bartender was wiping down the counter. "Philly PD," Bell said, and both he and Karpinsky flashed their IDs.

"Vice?" the bartender asked in a bored voice.

A couple of beefy men, squeezed into jackets like sausages in too-tight skins and wearing ties around their necks were lounging at the other end of the bar. They stopped staring at the dancer on stage and watched the two cops intently.

"Homicide," Bell responded. "We know the victim was here somewhat recently, and we just want to ask a few routine questions."

The bartender cocked an eyebrow. "Murder, eh?" He tossed his towel aside and moved toward them, at the same time waving down the two goons at the other end. "Whadda ya got?"

Bell held out a headshot of Kevin that had been taken at the morgue. "Recognize him?"

The bartender, whose name-tag identified him as Vic peered at the photo with his dark, close-set eyes. "Yeah, I remember him. We don't usually get blacks in this joint, so he kind of...stood out." He studied the picture again. "What happened to him?"

"Sorry. That's classified," said Bell, tapping the corner of the picture on the bar. "What do you remember about his visit?"

"Oh, not much. Pretty uneventful. I mean, if it had been eventful, I'd remember, right? So I guess you could say it was the usual, I guess. Have a few drinks, look at the pretty girls, go home and jack off."

"Did he come in with anyone, or was he alone?"

"He came in with Reggie."

"Reggie?"

"Yeah, Reggie Durkin, one of our regulars. If I recall correctly, he brought the guy along to help him celebrate his birthday. He seemed to enjoy himself well enough."

Karpinsky piped in, "Did things get out of hand at all?"

"No," said Vic. "He was kinda quiet, polite. I got the feeling it was the first time he'd ever been to a place like that. Reggie even treated him to a private lap dance."

All of this correlates with Durkin's story, Bell reflected. So far, the only surprise was that Durkin was a frequent customer. "You say Durkin is a regular here?"

"Yep. Comes in a couple times a week, usually in the evenings, 'cause he likes to see Jenna."

"Jenna? Is she here now?"

"No. She has today off, but she'll be here tomorrow evening if you want to come back - 7:00 till closing. She usually gets here about 6:00 to get ready."

"Thanks. I'll do that." Bell stood up, and he and Karpinsky left the building, recoiling slightly as the bright sunshine hit their unsuspecting eyes.

While Bell was investigating the seedy world of gentlemen's entertainment, Nicole was questioning Brandi in the small office in the back of Durkin's Restaurant.

Brandi was surprised to see her but welcomed her into the cramped space. "Have you caught who killed Kevin yet?"

"I'm afraid not." Nicole crossed her legs.

Brandi eyed Nicole's black pinstriped slacks and crisp white blouse and pulled her cardigan sweater over her own top, purchased on the sale rack at Target. "I'm not quite sure what more I can do for you," she said. "I already told your partner everything I know, which isn't much."

"You didn't tell him that you had a thing for Kevin."

Brandi's cheeks flushed. "Who told you that?"

"Never mind who told me that. Is it true?"

"Yeah. So what?" she demanded. "Do you have a problem with that?"

"No. Why would I have a problem with that? I didn't even know the guy. Why so defensive, Brandi?" Nicole stared at her coolly until Brandi looked away.

"No reason," she mumbled. "It's just that some people still have a problem with whites and blacks mixing like that. Besides," she added, looking back at Nicole, "it's not like anything happened."

"He turned you down?"

"Why are you bothering to ask? It sounds like you probably know everything already." She muttered something about Lori and Wanda being bitches.

"Were you angry that he refused you?"

"I don't know if I'd say angry – upset, disappointed, and a little embarrassed, maybe. This may be the twenty-first century and all, but it's still hard for a girl to ask a guy out."

"You asked him out a few times, right? And the answer was always the same?"

"Yeah. Eventually I gave up. There's only so much humiliation a girl can take, right?" Her face fell.

"Were you so humiliated that you might have asked a few friends to teach him a lesson? That you might have even joked about that?"

"What?" Brandi's head snapped back up.

"You heard what I said. Were you so upset and humiliated that you might have asked a few friends to rough Kevin up a little – and things got out of hand?"

Brandi's breath came out in short gasps. "What the hell are you talking about? Ask someone to rough him up? Is this some kind of sick joke? I don't have to take this!" She rose quickly.

"Sit down." Nicole's voice was quiet but it carried a steely resolve that was unexpected by anyone who didn't know her.

Brandi's eyes widened, and she slowly sat down again, watching Nicole warily, like a child who'd been corrected in front of her whole kindergarten class.

Nicole leaned forward slightly. "Do you know Drew Nichols, Brandi?"

Brandi flinched slightly, but said nothing. "Well?"

"Why do you want to know?"

"Drew Nichols and a friend are the ones who gave Kevin the star treatment a couple weeks back. We're trying to decide if you already knew that."

Brandi's freckles stood out even more as the blood drained from her face. "What?" she whispered.

"That's right, and anyone who knows Drew more than just casually knows his extreme racist views." She waited as Brandi sat silently, digesting this new information with her head bowed. Nicole also noticed that the girl's hands were gripped together tightly, her knuckles whitening.

"Yes," she said slowly. "I...I know him. I know Drew."

"How well do you know him? Are you friends or what?"

"I met him at a bar, and I was a little toasted at the time," she admitted. "We dated for a bit, but that was before I knew what a total creep he is. I broke it off after a few weeks. That was over a year ago. I swear I had no idea that he was one of the guys who bothered Kevin." Her eyes filled with tears.

Coincidences bother cops, and Nicole was no exception to this rule. She'd met more than her fair share of witnesses capable of crocodile tears. Her brows drew together slightly and she tapped her pencil on her notebook. "Did he know you work here?"

"Yes, but-"

"Let me see if I can get this straight. You dated a skinhead who was involved in a racial incident with a man who works with you? The same man who turned down your requests for dates? The same man who's the victim of a homicide. Hmm, seems a bit ironic, a bit coincidental, don't you think? Am I missing something here?"

"Please, you have to believe me. I had nothing to do with this. I liked Kevin. I was disappointed that he didn't want to go out with me, but that's all. I didn't tell Drew about it. I haven't seen him since I broke it off with him and even if I had, I wouldn't have... I never..." She bit her knuckle.

Nicole rose from her chair. "We may have more questions for you, Brandi. Do us a favor and don't go anywhere for the next few days." She left Brandi sitting slumped in her chair, tears trickling down her cheeks. As she walked through to the dining area, she nearly bumped into a young, slender woman with short red hair.

"Oh, I'm sorry," the redhead said. Seeing that Nicole had just come from the back, she asked, "Hey, can you tell me if Brandi is here?" She craned her neck as she tried to look past Nicole to the office in back.

On a hunch, Nicole flashed her badge. "Who are you?"

Startled, the woman replied, "Jennifer Morris." She then clapped her hand over her mouth. "Why do you want to know? I didn't do anything."

Nicole's keen memory kicked in: Brandi had given that woman's name as her alibi the night of Kevin's murder. She steered Jennifer toward an empty table over the other woman's feeble protests. "I just need a minute of your time," Nicole assured her. "I'm investigating the murder of a man who worked here. Do you know anything about it?"

"Yeah, Brandi told me. That sucks, doesn't it? I met him a couple times. Nice guy."

"Brandi told my partner that the night of the murder she was with you. Can you verify that?"

"Let's see…last Friday, wasn't it? Brandi and I went to the movies. We saw that new one with Adam Sandler. I was disappointed. I thought it'd be better." Jennifer rummaged through her purse, extracted some lip gloss and applied it, then smacked her lips together afterward.

"Which showing did you attend?"

"I think 9 o'clock."

Nicole's mind worked quickly. *Most comedies are about an hour and a half, which, taking all of the annoying ads and previews into account, would get them out of the theater around 10:45 – the tail end of the time window of death estimated by the M.E.* "Did you go anywhere afterward?"

"Yeah. We met some friends at a club."

So much for that theory, Nicole thought. "Any stops on the way?"

"No. Wait…hold on. That's not right. I was driving, and Brandi asked if we could stop here real quick. She had left her favorite jacket here and wanted to grab it. It was chilly after the movie."

Nicole's heart rate quickened. "When she came inside, how long did she take to retrieve her jacket?"

"I don't know. Ten minutes? Fifteen maybe? I remember I was annoyed because she took so long, but she told me that old fart Durkin had some questions for her."

"Did you see her go in or come out?"

"I wasn't really paying that much attention." Jennifer frowned. "What are you implying, anyway?"

Nicole stood up. "Thanks, Jennifer. That'll be all for now. If you're looking for Brandi, she's in the office." She strode out of the restaurant, leaving Jennifer gaping after her.

Drew Nichols was fully processed in the Detention Unit. By the time he was finished, the drugs in his system had dissipated. The unit corporal called upstairs, and Bell made his way downstairs.

"Do you want me to go with you?" Nicole asked.

"No, I'm okay," Bell replied. "I'll have a corrections officer come with me when I bring up Mr. Personality."

Nichols was brought out of the main holding cell and placed alongside the corridor wall. When Bell approached, Drew rolled his eyes.

"What say you and I have a little chat?" Bell said.

"Why should I?" spat Drew.

"Because it will give you a chance to tell your side of the story - you know, maybe explain why you had a fully-loaded Glock by your pillow and half of Colombia in your house?"

"I got nothing to say to you, cop," Drew retorted.

"Okay, but you have been through this enough times to know that the District Attorney's Office sometimes smiles upon those who cooperate; especially in a homicide case," Bell said.

"I already told you I didn't ice that nigger!" Drew nearly screamed. "Hell, I'd probably brag about it if I did!"

"Fine," Bell replied. "Then let's get your statement on the record."

Drew Nichols didn't like cops, but he knew how the system worked. In Philadelphia, there was a better-than-average chance he would get probation for the pistol and the drugs, even with the amount of heroin stashed in his home. *Hell*, Drew thought, *if this Bell character had found my secret stash, this case would have gone Federal. Thank God for those loose floorboards in the dining room.*

"Alright," Drew finally said. "Let's go."

Nichols was seated in an interrogation room when Ellis entered.

"Hey, baby." Drew smiled. "You miss me?"

"Yeah, like I'd miss fleas," she snapped back.

Bell smirked and gave Nichols the usual treatment. "Drew, are you left or right-handed?"

"Yes."

"Which one, smart-ass?" Bell said, releasing a sigh.

Drew smirked. "Right-handed."

Bell walked toward him and cuffed his left hand. This kept the suspect somewhat secure, but left his writing hand free to sign any interviews or confessions. The suspect would not be given a pen until after the interrogation was over; it was not a Hollywood exaggeration for Hannibal Lecter to use a pen as a deadly weapon and the police were keenly aware of this. "Let me check those cuffs for you," Bell said. He then squeezed them until Drew let out a whimper.

"That's too tight, asshole!" Drew yelled.

Nicole saw what her partner was doing but chose to ignore it for the moment. She followed a cardinal rule of not getting rough with prisoners, and it was a topic on which she and her partner often disagreed.

She asked Drew, "Do you want anything to eat or drink?"

"Sure," Drew replied. "How about a Coke?"

"You got it," she replied. "Be back in a minute."

After his partner left the room, Bell began preparing the necessary paperwork for the interrogation. The standard form was a 75-331, and its template was on every Detective Division computer. Bell, however, always wrote out his interrogations in longhand. It took longer to complete, but he believed that a hand written statement had more impact on a jury than a sterile computer form. Just to cover all the bases, Nicole usually typed the interrogation onto a computer-based 331.

Of course, nothing would be asked until Drew was read his Miranda rights. Unlike the warnings given on those allegedly "realistic" television crime dramas, real-life Mirandas are slightly more detailed. Sometimes Bell wished he could read them like Chief Wiggum once had in an early episode of *The Simpsons:* "You have the right to remain silent, anything you say blah, blah, blah, blah…"

Instead, when Nicole returned, Bell read the canned version to Nichols, an action he had done hundreds of times in his career, reading directly off the interrogation form:

"My name is Detective Bell and this is Detective Ellis from the Homicide Division – Philadelphia Police Department. We are questioning you concerning the violation of the Uniform Firearms Act (VUFA) and the discovery of narcotics inside your Disston Street residence. We have a duty to explain to you and to warn you that you have the following legal rights…"

You have a right to remain silent and do not have to say anything at all.

Anything you say can and will be used against you in court.

You have a right to talk to a lawyer of your own choice before we ask you any question and also to have a lawyer here with you while we ask questions.

If you cannot afford to hire a lawyer and you want one, we will see that you have a lawyer provided to you, free of charge, before we ask you any questions.

If you are willing to give us a statement, you have a right to stop any time you wish.

Drew seemed to be following the Miranda warnings and appeared to be coherent enough to answer questions.

Bell moved forward.

"Okay, Drew, I am going to ask you a few questions about the rights I just read. I need an answer of either 'yes' or 'no,' alright?"

"Yeah."

"Do you understand that you have a right to keep quiet and do not have to say anything at all?"

"Yes," Drew said.

"Do you understand that anything you say can and will be used against you?"

"Yes."

"Do you want to remain silent?"

"Yes."

Bell's eyebrows rose. "You want to remain silent, or do you want to talk to us?"

"I mean no. I want to talk to you, so my answer to the question is no. I got confused," Nichols said.

"Okay, no problem. That happens a lot," Nicole said, and it was the truth. Many defendants are so worried during an interview that they go on answer overdrive, sometimes saying "yes" to anything and everything without realizing it.

Bell continued, "Do you understand that you have a right to talk with a lawyer before we ask you any questions?"

"Yes."

"Do you understand that if you cannot afford to hire a lawyer, and you want one, we will not ask you any questions until a lawyer is appointed for you free of charge?"

"Yes." It was like listening to a broken record.

"Do you want to talk with a lawyer at this time or to have a lawyer with you while we ask you questions?"

"No," Drew snarled. "The last time my lawyer 'helped' me, I got sent to Graterford Prison."

"Are you willing to answer questions of your own free will, without force or fear, and without any threats or promises having been made to you?"

"Yes."

"Okay," Bell said. "Before we start the interview, I need you to read the questions I just asked you and the responses you have given. If everything is correct, sign your initials next to each answer."

Drew read the Miranda warnings and initialed his responses accordingly. When he was finished, Bell drew a slanted line from the top right of the page to the lower left. This was to ensure that the detectives would not change or add any answers to the questions given. He asked Drew to sign his full name on that line. Police can never be too careful about Miranda, as far too many rock-solid cases are thrown out on technicalities, so it was imperative that Nichols's understanding be made perfectly clear. The initials after the answers and the full name across the cover page helped to ensure that. There will always be defense attorneys who argue that their client did not understand the warnings or forced to sign the 75-331 under duress, but that is a judicial matter.

Once the Miranda rights were squared away, Bell began his questioning. Nothing would be written down at first, because it is easier for him to watch Drew's face and judge emotions if he didn't have to focus jotting down details. Bell and Nicole liked to have a conversation first, then go word by word after that. Thus far, it had proven to be their recipe for success.

Bell was the lead during this interview, so he began. "Okay, Drew, tell us about the gun."

"What gun?"

Bell immediately jumped up and slapped him in the back of the head. "Listen, you little asshole, if you think you are going to jerk us off today, you are sadly mistaken. I'll beat you within an inch of your miserable life and throw you down the goddamn elevator shaft. And believe me, you miserable, pathetic junkie lowlife, you will not be missed. Are we clear?"

"Yeah," Drew murmured.

"ARE WE CLEAR?" Bell repeated, sounding like a military drill sergeant.

"Yeah, we're clear. Jesus, take it easy." Drew was visibly shaken. While Bell probably wouldn't have beaten a suspect, he had a knack for making toads believe he would. He considered it an advantage.

He finally calmed down and asked, "Now, tell me about the gun."

"It's mine, all right? I bought it off a guy down in Kensington, somewhere around A and Somerset Streets - some wetback who told me he recently 'acquired' it."

"Acquired? From where?" Bell asked.

"He didn't say, dude, and I didn't ask." Drew responded. "All I know is that the cops took my last piece, and I needed some firepower. A .45 was just the thing."

"And let me guess… You had no idea that the serial number was filed off?" Bell asked.

"I knew. To be honest, I didn't fucking care. I was more concerned with having backup in case I ran into some trouble on the street. It's a dangerous city, ya know?"

"Yeah, we know," Nicole said wryly.

Bell continued, "Okay, how about the drugs? Enlighten me."

"So I had a little weed. Who doesn't? Hell, even the president gets away with firing up a fatty these days. God bless America."

Bell stifled a smile because he knew Drew was right. He was a toad, but he was right. Times had certainly changed since the days of Theodore Roosevelt, and maybe not for the better.

"Fair enough about the weed," Bell responded. "The heroin is another story though."

"Dude, that's not mine," Nichols lied. "The gun and the weed, yeah, but I don't touch that heroin crap. I seen too many people drop dead from that shit."

Twice in one day this asshole is right about something? Must be some kind of record, Bell thought. The heroin in Philadelphia is infamously pure; in 2000, it had the highest purity in the land. Many abusers overdose because their bodies cannot handle the reaction of Philly heroin. Local media outlets would usually decry this heroin as "tainted" or "bad," but in reality, it is very, very good - too good for a lot of people, it would seem.

Not that that was an issue for Bell. The detective took a hard line when it came to drug abusers, especially after losing a friend to an overdose. Years of begging, pleading, and threatening did no good, and when they'd found Tom dead in a bathroom with a needle in his arm, Bell had felt nothing – not sadness, not remorse, nothing at all. He'd refused to go to Tom's funeral, and he'd tried to purge every memory of him from his mind. Cold? Yes, but Bell was not about to be saddled with the guilt his other friends felt over Tom's fate. He had tried desperately to get Tom to listen to reason, and he'd received in return was scorn. *Screw him and anyone else who goes down that dark path.* That was Bell's final decision and his lifelong opinion of drug users.

Bell continued, "Well, if the heroin isn't yours, whose is it? We found it in your house…or at least it's your house until your mother gets out of jail. Are you trying to tell me it's hers?"

Drew bristled at the thought. His mother Jane had some problems, mostly with alcohol, but she was definitely not a drug abuser. As disappointing a son as he was to her, he was not about to throw her under the bus.

"No, it's not hers," Drew said. "With so many people coming in and out of the house, who knows? It could be anyone's. Look, I told you about the gun and the weed, but the heroin is not mine. Honest."

Bell couldn't tell if Drew was bullshitting or not, although the detective was getting the impression that he was lying. In the grand scheme of things, though, it didn't matter. Drew was going to be pinched for the pistol and the marijuana, and he was still the prime suspect in Kevin Myers's murder. *Speaking of which…*

"Drew, why don't you regale us with the story about the Myers incident? You remember…the fight at Durkin's Restaurant?"

"Jesus Christ!" Drew exclaimed. "This again? Like I already told you guys, I was in the restaurant with my friends. We were walking up and down South Street, taking in the sights and staring at some ass. That place hasn't been the same since Zipperhead closed down."

Zipperhead was a punk rock store that featured clothing, accessories, and memorabilia. It is mentioned in the 1988 song "Punk Rock Girl" by The Dead Milkmen, whose band members also hail from the City of Brotherly Love. Every Philadelphian Bell's age had been in the store at least once; in Bell's case, many times. Nicole didn't know it, but Detective John Bell was a big fan of The Dead Milkmen.

Drew kept going. "After walking around for a while, we wanted to grab some cheesesteaks before taking off. We stopped at Durkin's because Jim's Steaks was mobbed."

"That's the price you pay for having the best cheesesteaks in the city," Bell said. He'd always loved Jim's, sans the crowds.

"Fucking-A, right?" Drew replied. "Anyway, we grabbed a table, and some broad took our order. She was waitress hot."

"Waitress hot?" Nicole asked, eyebrows raised.

"Yeah, you know - compared to your average 'waitress,' on a scale of one to ten, she was about a nine. Compared to everyone else, she was about a five," Drew explained.

Wow, Nicole thought, *the criminal mind at work.*

"Go on," Bell said.

"Okay, so the waitress takes our order and disappears," Drew began. "She comes back a few minutes later with our drinks. About ten minutes after that, she brings the food over. It wasn't great, but it wasn't bad, and we ate our food while shooting the shit. Pretty soon we need refills on the drinks, and the broad brings them over. That was when it happened."

"What happened?" Bell asked.

"God. When that nigger spilled the drinks on us."

"Kevin Myers spilled the drinks on you?" Bell asked.

"No! The waitress was carrying the tray of drinks. The Myers guy was bussing the table next to us and bumped into her. It must have been a hard enough bump to make her spill her drinks on us," Drew said.

"Are you sure the waitress didn't spill the drinks on you because you guys were being loud and rude?" Nicole asked.

"And give up her tip?" Drew asked. "Not a chance. Look, lady, you probably won't believe this, but we weren't shouting 'nigger' in the diner. We were just talking. Shit, we weren't even that loud at first - not until the monkey gave us a soda bath. Besides, the waitress was white and Myers was black. There's no question which one was the savage."

Bell considered saying something to Drew about the racist remarks, but he thought better of it. Instead, he would dutifully write down every one of Nichols's racist rants; if it came down to that statement being read to a jury, any sympathy given this moron would go right out the window. He'd learned it's always best to hang criminals with their own words.

"So," Bell asked, "what happened next?"

"My friends and I jumped up and got in his face. We were pretty fucking pissed and started screaming at him. I think I said something like, 'What's your fucking problem, nigger? I oughtta kick your fucking monkey ass!'"

"And now Myers is dead." Bell said.

"Yeah, and if ya ask me, the world is better off for it. But as I told you before, I didn't kill him, and neither did any of my friends." Drew stated emphatically. "If we were gonna kill him, we woulda done it that night, not a few weeks later. Luckily for him, self-control got the better of me. After all, it was only soda, right? Who gives a fuck? Wasn't like he put his grimy hands on me or nothin'."

Bell wanted to argue that point, but Drew's story made sense. If they were going to kill Kevin Myers, they would have done it in the heat of the moment. Few people kill a man over spilled drinks, and even fewer kill a man a week after the fact. *Nichols may be a racist piece of garbage, but he isn't a psychopath. He hasn't got the brain power.* Unfortunately, that little fact put the detectives back to square one.

"Did anyone throw a punch or touch Myers in any way that night?" Bell asked.

"No, man." Drew said. "We pointed at the guy and screamed a lot, but that was it. A second or two after that, the slob of a manager waddled his fat, greasy ass out there and threatened to call the cops. We figured it was best to beat feet after that. I was home an hour later."

Bell was getting angry, not only because of Drew's responses, but because he was realizing that the toad was most likely not the man responsible for Myers's death. He was still a suspect, of course, but at that point, a murder charge wouldn't get past the district attorney. *No way.*

"Look, I told you I didn't do it," Drew said with a nasty grin. "You're just wasting everyone's time here."

When Bell saw Drew's yellowed smile, something inside of him snapped. He stood up and punched Drew in the face, knocking his head back.

"Do you think it's funny, motherfucker? Do you?" Bell screamed.

"What the fuck is the matter with you?" Drew cried.

Nicole rushed over and grabbed Bell. She used every ounce of strength to pull him off the druggie, and quickly shoved him out of the room. Many of the other detectives had heard the skirmish but it was par for the course; when they realized that Bell and Nicole were okay, they went back to their desks.

"What the hell is the matter with you, John?" Nicole asked angrily.

"Nothing. What is wrong with you?"

"Are you kidding me? You struck a *cuffed* prisoner. Are you out of your damned mind?"

Bell, still breathing heavily, replied, "No, I'm fine, but I'm not going to sit there while he laughs at us. He knows we can't charge him, and he's fucking laughing about it! Laughing at us while we're out here busting our asses trying to put the pieces together!"

Nicole looked into Bell's eyes and said quietly, "So what, John? We're better than him. You're better than him. Drew Nichols is not worth your career, and he certainly is not worth our partnership. But I'll tell you this. If something like that happens again, I'm out. Do you understand? I cannot and will not work with someone who hits a prisoner. Now calm down, compose yourself, and get back in there and act like an officer of the law."

"Okay," Bell said.

A few minutes later, the pair reentered the interrogation room. Bell and Nichols stared at each other for a few uncomfortable minutes before Nicole broke the silence with a question.

"Drew, do you have anything else to add to your statement?"

"You mean besides the police brutality?" Drew asked.

"You think I care about that, Drew?" Nicole asked. "If you want to go that route, to file a complaint, that's not a problem. Heck, we'll bring you the form right now and turn it in for you, but any courtesy you would receive for this interview goes right out the window. The choice is yours."

"Never mind. It's not like a cop is going to believe me anyway." Drew paused. "You'll tell the D.A. that I cooperated, right?" he asked.

"Yeah. We'll submit this interview to them with your case file and arrest paperwork," Bell said. "We're going to go over your story one more time so I can get everything down on paper. After that, I'll let you read the entire interview for accuracy, and if it's okay, you'll need to sign and date the bottom of each page."

Drew nodded agreement and retold the story. When he was finished, he checked the interview, made a few small changes, and signed and dated the indicated pages.

Since he was already angry, Bell smiled and slipped in a parting shot. "Oh, and Drew, you are still a suspect in the Myers murder, so when you get out, don't make any travel plans. We're taking your pistol to the Firearms Identification Unit, and they are going to run a ballistics test. If your gun matches the bullet we found in Kevin Myers, you'll be spending your Christmas on death row. Got it?"

"Yeah, I got it," Drew shot back.

"Good," Bell said.

The detectives knew full well that Myers had not been shot, but Drew Nichols didn't know that. The official cause of death had not been released to the media and probably would not be until a suspect was charged. Two corrections officers were called upstairs to take Drew back to his cell. Bell and Nicole stayed in the interrogation room, and when they were sure Drew was on the elevator, Bell erupted.

"FUCK! FUCK! FUCK!" he screamed before punching the table with all his might. "Son of a bitch! We're back to square fucking one!" As if to punctuate the last sentence, Bell kicked his chair across the room.

Nicole has seen this kind of explosion from Bell before. He was good for one every six months or so. Bell's problem, in her opinion, was that he kept everything bottled up inside, until he couldn't take it any longer. Then something would set him off, and six months of anger, disappointment, and guilt would come out in an unusual – for him – profanity-laced tirade, like some kind of bi-annual case of Tourette syndrome. The detectives in the unit, and even Sergeant Baker, knew this and rarely batted an eye when it happened. There were rumors that an office pool had been set up around Bell's outbursts, but so far the tally board had not been discovered.

"It's okay, John," Nicole explained. "We'll get this guy. The case hasn't gone cold, so we'll just keep trudging along until someone makes a mistake."

Still breathing heavily, sweat dripping from his brow, Bell sheepishly agreed. "I know, Nic," he said. "I'm sorry about that. I just couldn't help myself."

"I know," Nicole said. "You think I didn't want to beat the hell out of him, too? The guy is scum, but he's sitting in a jail cell thanks to you…well, to us, I guess." Nicole smiled, and that was usually the spark that changed Bell's mood for the better.

"Thanks. You're a good friend and an even better partner. Let's get back to work. We owe that to Kevin Myers."

Chapter Nine

After having dealt with the dregs of society in the interview room, Bell and Nicole decided they needed a booze break before heading home. Neither of them were really big drinkers, but sometimes it took a cold one to wash away the dirty feeling that clung to them during an investigation like that one that seemed to drag on and on.

Nicole drove and dropped Bell off at the entrance of their favorite hangout in Mayfair. The plan for him was to grab a couple seats and hold them until she could park the car. The Call Box was a popular hangout for cops – a place to decompress and relax with friends and colleagues. Owned by a retired cop, it was named after the old "call box" system that allowed the police to call for an ambulance in case of an accident; that was back at the turn of the twentieth century. Mayfair was a solid neighborhood and a popular one for bars. There was one on just about every corner, and they ran the gamut from dives to swank establishments. Part of the allure of The Call Box was that because it wasn't one of the glitzier spots in the area, the upscale "party hearty" crowd tended to go elsewhere, and because it was a known cop magnet, the seedier element steered clear.

The bar was usually quite busy in the afternoon and evening hours, and Bell and Nicole's favorite table was not always available, but they happened to get lucky. Bell ordered a couple beers on his way in – Corona for him, Heineken for her – and made a beeline for a table tucked into a corner of the bar, which was already buzzing with activity.

Knowing that Bell was waiting, Nicole found a parking spot as close to The Call Box as she could.

As she made her way to the entrance, she was hailed by a youngish man wearing jeans and a lime-green polo shirt. "Hey, babe, can you recommend somewhere good to get a drink?"

Nicole noticed a couple of weenie-looking guys sniggering nearby, obviously his idiot friends.

"Sure. Why don't you try Smokie's?" Smokie's Pub, owned and operated by a former Philly fireman, was one of the more popular establishments in Mayfair - that and it was a good two blocks away from The Call Box.

"I was thinking more along the lines of this place. Whaddaya say? How's about joining me? You won't get a better offer this decade." He hitched up his jeans and glanced over his shoulder at his friends, who waited breathlessly for Nicole to fall for his pathetic pickup line.

Tossing her blonde head back in what she assumed was a provocative manner, Nicole smiled. She then put her hands on her hips, an action that pushed back the bottom of her blazer and exposed the gun and badge resting on her hip.

Mr. Smooth's eyes goggled as he looked down.

"You were saying?" she said curtly.

"Er, uh…" he mumbled.

"Beat it, before I arrest you."

"On what grounds?"

"For being a total ass." She didn't even wait for him to stumble away, red-faced, before entering The Call Box. As her eyes adjusted to the dim light, she saw Bell waving at her from their spot at the back. She pushed her way through the crowd, greeting familiar faces as she passed. She finally plopped down at the table next to Bell and grabbed the proffered beer.

"What the hell took you so long? Nothing's nastier than warm beer, you know."

"Sorry. Just had to fend off some drunken frat boy idiot who tried to pick me up." Nicole looked at the beer. As much as she wanted it, she knew she shouldn't. "Listen, I'm not much in the mood for beer. Sorry. I'll be right back." She made her way to the bar and ordered plain seltzer with lemon.

"What, are you on the wagon?" Bell asked once his dropped mouth was able to function again.

"No. I'm just…not in the mood for beer. I guess I should have told you before you ordered it. Sorry."

Normally he could worm just about anything out of Nicole, but something in her tone warned Bell to lay off the interrogation for the time being.

"Okay, no problem," he said easily. "I'll drink it myself."

They clinked bottle and glass and drank in silence. Bell watched Nicole slump back in her chair and relax, a rarity for her when on the job. She was always on point, always focused. Nicole was one of the few women in Homicide, and he knew as well as she did that she had to prove herself twice over. She never gave any of the guys a chance to put one over on her. She never complained or whined when things got tough, as they invariably did in their grisly line of work, and that was admirable of her, especially since she worked in a culture dominated by men.

When on a case, the two of them spent more time together than she and her husband Jeff did. Bell knew Jeff and liked him; he also knew Jeff was confident in his relationship with Nicole and didn't feel threatened by her close professional involvement with another man. That was another thing that had bugged Renee. She was sure there was something more to Bell and Nicole's relationship than a police partnership, and toward the end she'd even had the gall to accuse him of having an affair with Nicole.

He'd laughed in her face at the absurdity of such a suggestion, but every now and again – like when he'd caught that "interesting" view of her during the search of Drew's house – he couldn't help thinking what it would be like to come home to someone as beautiful, independent, and compassionate as Nicole. It wasn't a thought he'd ever dwell upon for too long, however. Fraternizing with colleagues of the opposite sex was frowned upon by the Philly PD, married or not. Besides that, Bell respected her too much to even think of such a possibility.

While Bell was brooding, Nicole was involved in her own thoughts. Ironically, they were somewhat similar to Bell's – something that would have surprised him had he known. While she was deeply in love with Jeff, there were times when she, too, wondered what it would be like to have a more intimate relationship with Detective John Bell. She knew he'd been terribly hurt by Renee's defection and, as his friend and partner, she naturally sided with him. Nicole hadn't been too impressed with Renee while she and Bell were dating, so being supportive after the breakup hadn't been difficult. Still, she knew his habit of keeping certain aspects of his life walled away from the people who cared could frustrate anyone, even someone with more depth than the feckless Renee.

Nicole toyed with her half-empty glass. With his short, dark hair, hazel eyes, chiseled features, and slim, muscular build, there was no denying that Bell was a looker. He could have had just about anyone with merely a crook of his finger, but he was far more complicated than that. John Bell was not a "one-night-stand" kind of guy. She knew a little about his childhood, which seemed like a lonely one, and she also knew he was looking for someone with whom he could really share a life. Trouble was, whenever he found someone, he had difficulty with the sharing part. She suddenly found herself wondering what kind of father Bell would make, and she didn't know how to feel about wondering that.

The two of them were jolted out of their parallel reveries by the arrival of Brian Karpinsky and Bill King, who had been helping them out on the Myers case. "Hey, why the long faces?" Brian called out as the two men pulled up a couple empty chairs and sat down, turning the table from cozy to crowded. "Didn't you have that little prick Drew Nichols in for questioning today?"

Bell sighed. "Yeah, but it wasn't the slam dunk we were hoping for." He then related the relevant portions of the interview, leaving out the part about the fact that he almost killed the junkie.

Bill whistled. "Damn. Tough break."

"Well, he's not completely off the hook yet," Nicole reminded them, "Still, it's not looking too much like he's the one who did it." She paused. "John scared the crap out of him though. It was a joy to behold."

"Meh, it's one of the few perks of the job, right?" Bill winked, and Nicole smiled back.

Detectives Karpinsky and King were both older than Bell and Nicole by about fifteen years. Closer to retirement age, neither of them truly wished to be promoted any further. Bill King was a bit stout in the middle and sported a receding hairline, and his easy manner made him a favorite of cops of all ages. Plus, he was expecting his first grandchild, which contributed to his being more genial than usual.

Brian Karpinsky, on the other hand, was a little pricklier in his manner. It was common knowledge, though, that he was stuck in a rather long and unhappy marriage but refused to separate or divorce for religious reasons. There were rumors of the fit, attractive older man having affairs, but that was all they were: unsubstantiated rumors. In spite of their differences in age and demeanor, the four detectives had worked together on various cases over the years, and they got along reasonably well. Bill and Brian were among only a handful of cops in Homicide who didn't give Nicole flak on a daily basis, and she and Bell both appreciated that, as the problem was more endemic among the older men.

"So what've we got?" Brian asked, swigging from his bottle of Budweiser.

"Like Nicole said, Drew Nichols may have been our main suspect, but he's not off the hook yet. There's still the possibility that Brandi, the assistant manager of the restaurant who was romantically spurned by the victim, enlisted Nichols to beat him up, and maybe things got out of hand. Apparently, this Brandi dated Nichols for a short time."

"God, it's like daytime television, *The Young and the Restless*, Philly edition. What do women see in that Drew character anyway?" mocked Nicole.

"Hey, don't knock that show. My wife's a big fan," Bill teased.

"And," Nicole continued, ignoring Bill's interjection, "the night of the murder, Brandi and a friend went to the movies and then to a club."

"So, she has an alibi, right?"

"Well, maybe, but I found out that on the way from the theater to the club, they stopped at Durkin's to get Brandi's sweater. The friend who was driving said Brandi was in there for quite some time, an estimated ten or fifteen minutes, and she didn't see Brandi go in or out. Brandi's friend said Durkin held her up, but still, I think-"

"Interesting." Bell had finished his Corona and was shaking the spent lime slice inside the bottle. "Who knows what she was really doing? Calling Drew? Luring Kevin to his fate?" He thought of the alleyway behind the building where the restaurant and apartment above were located. While it wasn't a major thoroughfare, drivers occasionally used it as a shortcut, and delivery trucks likely parked back there too. *Wait, they found motor oil on Kevin's shirt. Could he have been murdered so close to home?* The prospect was chilling.

Gradually, the talk turned to sports – particularly how the Flyers were faring in the NHL playoffs and how the Phillies had stumbled in early season play – and other pop culture topics. Eventually Bill and Brian rose to leave, and Bell and Nicole followed shortly after. Nicole dropped Bell off at Homicide to retrieve his car, and then she headed home as Jeff had promised to have dinner waiting. Bell, on the other hand, drove off to his bachelor pad for either takeout or a microwave meal.

A short time later, Nicole pulled up in front of the home she shared with Jeff in Somerton. They'd only been there a year, and getting the place up to their preferred living standards was taking time, considering they both had busy careers. The Somerton section is located in the far northeast part of the city, just west of U.S. Route 1 (known as Roosevelt Boulevard within the city limits) and east of the borders of both Montgomery and Bucks Counties. The always-congested Bustleton Avenue splits the neighborhood down the middle, and most residents do whatever they can to avoid "The Gaza Strip." Nicole despised that term, since the nickname is a slam at the section's large Jewish population. She learned immediately that if anyone had a problem with immigrants, Somerton was not the place for them.

During a short trip to the supermarket, Nicole could pass a synagogue, an Indian catering business, and an Uzbekistani restaurant. Many of the strip malls along Bustleton Avenue have signs written in both English and Cyrillic, since the area's Russian population is even larger than the Jewish one, and while the area is diverse, it is almost completely without tensions. Violent crime is not much of a factor in Somerton, although Nicole was surprised to learn that the Russian mob is quite active in the area. She decided to keep that little tidbit to herself, since most of her neighbors would have an aneurysm if they ever found out. Besides, the Major Crimes Division tended to be all over the situation there, especially since the glory days of the Philadelphia Italian Mafia were long gone.

Nicole's street was a quiet, tree-lined slice of heaven. Like many streets in Somerton, police officers, firefighters, and other blue-collar municipal types occupied the homes around her. Bell, who'd first suggested the neighborhood to Nicole, called Somerton "the last bastion of decent living in this dreaded town." It also helped, he explained, that Somerton was the furthest north one could live without leaving the city. Philadelphia police personnel were mandated to live inside the city limits, thanks to a 1953 ruling. For the city, the rule was both a blessing and a curse. While the residency requirement keeps much of the tax base from getting out of Dodge, it also significantly minimizes the pool of new, qualified police recruits. Every recent academy class has had at least one recruit either dismissed or arrested because the department found out they were dealing drugs, beating their spouse, or worse. The residency requirement was recently repealed, but some of the other issues were still prevalent. Thankfully, that was not Nicole's problem anymore. At Homicide, she could pick and choose to interact with officers she and Bell trusted. *No way am I calling in some knucklehead cop to help serve a search warrant. Too damned risky.*

As Nicole walked up the steps to the front door, she scanned the front of her home and smiled. Her residence was a single split-level ranch style, with a full, finished basement and two above-ground floors. The home contained three bedrooms and one and a half bathrooms, more than enough space for their ultimate family plan. The backyard was rather large, and it was Jeff's deciding factor when choosing to buy, although he cursed that decision when it came time to mow the lawn. She and Jeff were only the second to own the home, as they purchased the residence from an elderly Hungarian woman. While the house needed some modern cosmetic improvements, everything else was in tiptop shape. All in all, it was a terrific place to live.

She walked in and inhaled deeply, loving the aroma instantly – Jeff had put a stew in the crock pot that morning and the scent was heavenly. He was in the process of pulling rolls out of the oven when she entered the kitchen. She waited for him to put the baking sheet on the counter before grabbing him and giving him a long, deep kiss.

"Well, hello there," Jeff said. "And to what do I owe this honor?" He hadn't completely changed out of his work clothes; he had shed the jacket and tie but was still wearing slacks and a white button-down shirt. Jeff, thirty-six, worked as a lawyer for a company that provided technological services to other businesses. He'd started out at law school thinking perhaps he might like to give back to society by working as a defense lawyer (the ones appointed for the defendants who could not afford a lawyer), but an internship with the State of Pennsylvania had opened his eyes and he decided to go into corporate law. Some of his more liberal friends had scorned what they called his "capitalist leanings," but he didn't care.

What did bother him – at least a little – was Nicole's close working relationship with John Bell. Had she been paired with another woman or even a much older, married man with a pot belly and thinning hair, Jeff would not have given her partner a second thought. But Bell was still undeniably young and attractive. Also, he had that brooding personality lightened just enough by a good sense of humor, enough to attract women like moths to the proverbial flame. It wasn't that Jeff didn't trust his wife, but no red-blooded man could ignore the possibility of his spouse straying when such an attractive alternative was so close at hand; especially since she saw more of her partner than she did of him during their frequent, intense cases.

The thing was, Jeff actually liked Bell. Not only had he and Nicole socialized with John Bell and Renee, but after Bell and Renee broke up, they continued hanging out with Bell. He was a real guys' guy, someone a fella could talk to about sports, politics, or just about any other topic. The one good thing about it was that Jeff knew he could trust Bell – enough to watch his wife's back in what was a very dangerous profession. So he kept his niggling concern buried, and he was confident that Nicole had no idea it existed. She had enough to worry about on the job without knowing that her husband sometimes had disturbing visions of she and Bell entangled in some romantic clinch.

A few minutes of silence ensued as the two of them dished up stew and sat down at the kitchen table. As they began eating, Jeff inquired about Nicole's day. "Any break in the case?"

"No." She sighed, bringing him as up to date as she could without divulging more than she should to an outsider. "The kid's a creep, but we need a lot more than what we've got if we're going to get an arrest warrant. We haven't discounted the possibility that he might have been in cahoots with the chick who works at the diner, but so far, we have no real proof that either of them was involved."

"Still digging then?"

"Yeah. Say, I get enough shop talk at work." Nicole pushed aside her plate. Her appetite was a bit off, but she was afraid he'd ask her why she wasn't eating, and she wasn't quite ready to break the news to him yet that he was going to be a daddy a bit earlier than they'd planned. She stood up, grabbed his hand and began dragging him toward the bedroom. "Let's do something else." *Anything to keep my mind off what I'm avoiding telling him.*

"Um, I was planning on watching the game tonight."

"That's what DVR is for," she replied, winking at him.

"You're right. What the hell? Besides, I can catch the instant replays online tomorrow."

Hand in hand, they raced toward the bedroom.

It was Tuesday morning, and Bell arrived at HQ a little worse for wear. He'd had another annoying call from his mother, which had prompted him to swig down a few more beers while watching some lame reality show on television. On top of that, he hadn't slept well due to indigestion from the Chinese takeout he'd devoured at dinner. When his *moo goo gai pan* kept threatening to come up for a second visit in the middle of the night, he'd decided he'd finally heed his friends' warnings about the Panda Palace.

Thus, to arrive and be confronted by a gaggle of people yelling and shouting was more than just off-putting; it was enough to make him lose his temper - almost. He managed to keep it in check when he saw Sergeant Baker amongst them.

Baker pushed to the front of the group and pulled him aside, just as Bell noticed Leon and Norma Myers were part of the fray.

"What the hell is going on?" Baker barked.

"I don't know, sir. I just walked in."

"Well you'd better figure it out. I don't have time for this crap."

"Can you explain, sir? Who are all these people?" Bell knew Baker hated it when he "sirred" him every other minute. *But what's he gonna do about it? Write me up for insubordination for using a title of respect?*

"All these people are representatives from Blaq Unity, and they want some answers on the Myers case…and so do his aunt and uncle." Like Bell, Baker had little use for most activist groups because he felt they created more problems than they solved, especially when it came to police work. No matter what Bell thought of him – and he knew Bell's opinion of him wasn't terribly high – Baker was loyal to the law and to the department, first and foremost. Unfortunately, being a black officer at the Philly PD meant that, in cases where blacks were concerned, he had "betrayed" either one side or the other. It wasn't an enviable position.

Bell knew this, of course, but it didn't make much difference to how he viewed his superior. Baker was always riding his ass about something, so he wasn't about to give an inch if he didn't have to. "We're doing our best, sir, but we aren't ready to make an arrest yet."

"Well, Bell, you'd better figure something out…and fast. The department can't afford to mess this one up." He started back toward his office. "Get these people out of here, will you?" he called back over his shoulder.

Bell started off after him, blood pounding in his ears, but he was grabbed by the arm by Nicole, whom he hadn't seen in all the chaos. "Don't do it," she hissed. "You know he's just waiting for you to start something."

"Okay, okay," he muttered. "You can let go now."

So far, the members of Blaq Unity had not seemed to notice him.

"What the hell is going on here? I thought Baker was going to handle them. What do they want? And why are Myers's aunt and uncle talking to them?"

"I don't know much more than you do, but I don't think the Myers folks came with them. I think they were already here when the aunt and uncle arrived."

"Well, I don't like the looks of it." He could see one man speaking earnestly with Leon Myers, whose face was definitely troubled. "Let's see if we can straighten these folks out. Call for a couple uniforms, will you?" He strode forward to address the group, which was comprised of about ten people including Leon and Norma Myers.

"Ladies and gentlemen, I'm Detective Bell, and this is the Homicide Division, not an off-track betting parlor. Unless you have specific business with us, I'll have to ask you to leave."

The man who had been speaking with Leon Myers shouted back, "We do have business with you, mister, and we ain't going nowhere!"

"Then please state the nature of that business so we can get back to work, back to serving the public." Bell wasn't quite successful in keeping a hint of sarcasm out of his voice.

The man pushed his way forward, cheered on by his compatriots. Wearing black jeans and a leather jacket, he looked like he was in his mid-forties. "I'm Jamal Taylor, and I represent Blaq Unity. We're here to talk about the Kevin Myers murder."

"Do you have any information that will help us find his killer?"

Taylor bristled. "Seems we should be asking you that question, Detective."

"Oh? My partner and I have been working nonstop on this case and this case alone since Friday night, but any-"

"Bullshit."

"Excuse me?"

"I said it's bullshit. Don't tell me you've been working on this case nonstop. Kevin was just another statistic, another black man down to you, isn't he? Who the hell cares who killed him or why, right? Why waste time and taxpayers' dollars on his case?" A group murmur of approval rose behind him, and he turned toward them and nodded.

Bell's temper threatened to flare up, but he caught Nicole's eye and took a deep breath before responding. "Mr. Taylor," he said slowly, "this is not a television show. In real life, murder cases are not solved in an hour. I assure you that we're devoting as many resources to this case as we possibly can, and we're doing our very best to solve it. Beyond that, I'm not at liberty to say anything to anyone unconnected with the case, so you'll have to read about it in the paper, just like everyone else."

"So you're saying you don't have any leads?" This came not from Taylor, but from a younger white woman who was standing slightly apart from the group. She wore a shapeless poncho and had a stenographer's notebook in her hand. *Damn*, Bell thought, recognizing it was Jean Gardner from *The Inquirer*. *Who the hell let her slither in here?*

"We're not prepared to make a statement at this time," Nicole butted in, saving Bell from his own tendency to swear at the press. "We're investigating every lead and every tip we receive. Beyond that, we've nothing to report. Thank you," she said, nodding to the two uniformed officers she'd requested. "Please follow Officers Blaylock and Kline, and they will show you out."

The Blaq Unity members grumbled, but they knew they were defeated for the moment.

Taylor glanced back as he was ushered toward the door. "You haven't heard the last from us!" he shouted.

Both Nicole and Bell ignored him as they made sure the Myerses were not herded out with Jean Gardner and the Blaq Unity members. As the others were led out, Bell could see Jean Gardner scribbling away furiously in her notebook, and he cursed under his breath. *Wednesday's edition should be an exciting one.*

"Is what they say true?"

Bell looked across the room to see Norma Myers standing there with tears streaming down her face.

"Of course not," he replied. "With all due respect, ma'am, groups like that have an agenda, and there isn't much we can say or do to persuade them otherwise. They'll exploit anyone and anything to prove their case or bolster their cause, and I'm afraid this includes your nephew's murder."

"Then where are the results?" Leon Myers was not weepy like his wife rather his voice held a steely undertone that hadn't been there the day before. Apparently, Jamal Taylor had had some success.

"Mr. Myers," Nicole said, "I can assure you we are doing everything we can. Each case is important and gets our full attention. We do not play favorites," she emphasized. "Not with anyone and certainly not because of anything having to do with race."

"Humph," Leon snorted. "We'll see."

A short while after they'd done their best to assure the deceased's aunt and uncle that they were doing all they could to find their nephew's murderer and sent the disgruntled couple on their way, Bell picked up the phone.

"Homicide. Bell here."

"Detective Bell? It's me, Emma Watson, from Durkin's."

"Well, hello, Ms. Watson."

"Please call me Emma."

"Okay, Emma. What can I do for you?"

"Well, you told me that if anything important came up, I should let you know."

"You have some information about the Myers case?"

"I'm not sure. Maybe, but I don't even know if it's relevant."

"Why don't you let me be the judge of that?" If Bell had had a dollar for every time someone questioned the importance of potential evidence, he'd have been a very wealthy man. As he pulled out a pad and pencil, he caught Nicole's eye and mouthed Emma's name.

"Okay." There was a slight pause during which Bell could hear traffic in the background and the annoying sound of wind blowing into the mouthpiece of a cell phone. "Well, um, this morning, Daryl and Lawrence didn't show up for work. Mr. Durkin seemed really upset about it."

"I imagine he would be, being caught shorthanded like that." Bell stifled a yawn and slumped down slightly in his chair.

"Yeah, maybe, but it's happened before…I mean, people not coming to work with no phone call. Obviously he gets mad about it, being the boss and all, but this time was different. He seemed – I don't know – almost frantic."

Bell sat up. "That's very, very interesting. Have those two skipped out on work before?"

"No, that's just it. They're usually pretty reliable. I can understand that Mr. Durkin would be upset, but he seemed more intense than usual. I've heard rumors that he hires kitchen help under the table, so maybe he's worried about being discovered by the IRS or something. I don't know. Oh, and before I hang up, there's something else."

"Shoot."

"Mrs. Durkin came in today."

"Is that unusual?"

"It's not unusual for her to stop by, but she doesn't usually come so early in the morning. When I went back to use the bathroom, I could hear them arguing in the office. I wasn't really trying to eavesdrop, you know, because I'm not the kind of person, but the walls are thin back there, and I couldn't help overhearing."

"Any idea what they were arguing about?"

"No, but she was saying something about not remembering, and he kept telling her to just stick to the story."

"Do they argue often that you know of?"

"Well, I don't know what things are like at home, but they don't usually argue when they're at the diner together. Maybe Mr. Durkin was still just upset about Daryl and Lawrence, but…well, I just don't know," Emma ended lamely.

Bell thanked her for the information, hung up, and quickly related the contents of the call to Nicole. They speculated for a few minutes on what exactly Reginald Durkin meant when he told his wife to "stick to the story," and they agreed that separate visits to each Durkin was in order – and soon.

The run-in with the Blaq Unity people had Bell in a mood, and when he finally cooled off, he remembered that he and Nicole were due in court that day. The Rockatansky trial was about to go to the jury, so Assistant District Attorney Thomas Kane would be making closing arguments; Kane's closings were never to be missed. The man was a brilliant orator, he knew how to play to an audience, and he was the only ADA in Philadelphia history with an urban legend attributed to him.

According to the story, back when Kane was the new hotshot in the Major Trials Division, the district attorney at the time, a despicable, petty politician -

wanted to knock Tom down a peg. Coincidentally, the trial of Malik Jefferson, accused of murdering a Philadelphia police officer, was about to begin. Jefferson had allegedly shot the female officer twice in the chest, and after she went down, he was accused of kicking her in the face so many times that he left her completely unrecognizable. If her nameplate hadn't survived the gunshots, the responding officer wouldn't have known who she was.

The good news for the D.A.'s office was that the murder was captured on video, courtesy of an intersection camera in the area of Broad Street and Germantown Avenue. The bad news was that while the description matched that of Jefferson, the camera never caught the killer's face. Everyone knew he had done it, but proving that beyond a shadow of a doubt was going to be difficult. Further complicating matters was the fact that Jefferson had never been arrested for anything other than shoplifting, and the murder weapon had been wiped clean. It was a case that would have been impossible to successfully prosecute, and the district attorney gleefully assigned it to the office's new golden boy.

That was a mistake.

Capitalizing on strong circumstantial evidence and a few defense miscues, Kane put up a terrific case that enthralled the media. It also seemed to convince the jury. The *coup de grace* came during closing arguments, when Kane sliced through Jefferson's defense like a surgeon, skillfully defeating alibi after alibi. He moved toward the officer's family and explained how the husband had missed the opportunity to kiss his wife goodbye that day, for he'd been working late at the office. Kane explained that the last time the son had seen his mother, the two had argued about school work and gone to sleep angry with each other. "Now, they'll never get the chance to tell her how much they loved her, how much they needed her, how much they were proud of her. And why? Because that chance was taken away by Malik Jefferson, a petty thug who murdered a police officer in cold blood."

Most of the gallery and many of the jurors were in tears, but Jefferson remained unmoved. That was fine, though, because Kane was "in the zone." He turned to Jefferson.

"Mr. Jefferson, I know about your mother. I know that by all accounts, she was a tremendous woman. Everyone loved her, respected her. I also know she was brutally beaten in a robbery a few years back. For that I am sorry. I am sorry our police could not help her that day. I am sorry that what is now my office could not punish her attacker with the jail time he so richly deserved. And I am sorry she recently passed away. I am sure you loved her very, very much. I understand that she was a churchgoer, a faithful woman who called upon the Lord for guidance and strength. She is with Him now, Mr. Jefferson, in a far better place than in the one we stand today. No matter the outcome of this trial today, I want you to ask yourself one simple question. Ask yourself, 'Is my mother proud of the person I have become?'"

That was all it took. Jefferson began to weep, and in minutes, he was crying hysterically. Looking at Kane, Jefferson quietly sobbed, "I did it. I killed that cop – that boy's mama. I am so very, very sorry."

Panic ensued. The gallery started shouting in disbelief.

The defense attorney began screaming his objections, while his client raised his voice to be heard: "I DID IT! I SHOT HER!" The judge immediately had the jury removed, and the courtroom cleared.

Kane just stood there, smiling.

The judge tried to instruct the jury to ignore Jefferson's comments, but the damage had already been done to the defense. The high-profile case would not end in a mistrial, and even if it did, the chances of finding an unbiased jury were almost nil.

A few weeks later, the jury came back with a guilty verdict, and Jefferson received a life sentence. Thomas Kane had accomplished the unimaginable; he'd won a case that had been deemed unwinnable. From that moment on, Kane received all the tough cases, and his conviction record remained the best in the state.

There was little chance of such dramatics in the Rockatansky case, but Bell and Nicole would be in attendance anyway. Of course, simply appearing court was an aggravating task all its own. The department had just recently entered the twentieth century in terms of technology, and the city was crowing about their new toy: fingerprint scanners. The scanners had recently been installed in every courtroom at the Criminal Justice Center, as well as every divisional court location. Police personnel would approach the keypad, type in their payroll number (the main identification number for city employees) and place their right index finger on the scan pad. The scanner would verify the officer's identity, and clock them in and out of each courtroom.

Bell hated the scanners, and often said to Nicole, "It's only a matter of time until they rise up against their human oppressors." He preferred the old way, the time-honored tradition of the punch clock: They'd just slip in the notice, stamp it with the date and time, and be on your way. "Easy –peasy, lemon squeezy," he'd say, prompting Nicole to roll her eyes.

Bell and Nicole stopped at the Court Attendance Unit, located inside City Hall. The detectives clocked in and made a beeline for the CJC across the street. While they technically could have skipped the punch-in since they were working the day-shift and not making overtime that day, the duo did things by the book, especially when Sergeant Baker was around. *Why give the knucklehead ammunition for the next argument?* When they came through the revolving doors of the center, Nicole sighed heavily.

"Damn it! I hate this system," she said.

The uninspired concrete behemoth had been built in 1994 as an alternative to the aging, obsolete City Hall courtrooms. The lobby was overflowing with victims, defendants, and potential jurors. Everyone had to go through the metal detectors, and that took a lot of time. There were four detectors in the lobby, and the CJC received thousands of visitors every day: do the math. Police personnel could skip the metal detectors, obviously, but even though they didn't have to wait in line, there was still a delay. The city, in its infinite wisdom, had only installed six elevators for the entire building. Six! So, once they made it through the metal detectors, they still had a thirty-minute wait for an elevator. It was madness. Many people took the stairs, but by the time they reached the fifth floor, they'd be calling for the oxygen. Even athletic types had trouble beating the dreaded CJC steps.

Thankfully, homicide trials were scheduled on the third floor. Bell and Nicole had no problem taking the escalator to the second floor and jogging up to the third. Like most police personnel, they ignored the dozens of people smoking in the stairwell right in front of the "No Smoking" signs. They knew if they made a big deal about one, they'd have to make a stink about them all, and many of the smokers were court employees: court criers, stenographers, and lawyers. It wasn't worth the hassle, but it was always worth it to sneer at the violators - at least it was for Nicole.

The pair opened the door to Courtroom 304 and saw Kane standing at the prosecutor's table. They caught his eye, and he walked over quickly. He shook Bell's hand and gave Nicole a quick hug.

"Hey, guys. How're things?" Kane asked.

"Hi, Tom," Nicole said. "The usual. We wanted to stop by for closings. How are we looking?"

"Well, I think it's a slam dunk, but you can't count on my humble opinion," Kane replied. "I always think that."

The Rockatansky case probably was a slam dunk though. The defendant had shot the victim three times in the back and dropped the pistol next to the body to make a statement. Unfortunately for Joe Rockatansky, technicians from the Crime Scene Unit were able to lift his prints from the murder weapon and the three spent shell casings left at the scene. Rockatansky made a statement all right, and that statement was, *"I'm an idiot."*

"Well, good luck anyway." Bell said, and the detectives found space on a bench in the back of the room.

ADA Kane began his closing arguments with the fingerprint evidence, and Nicole listened intently. It was always an honor to watch a genius at work, and she leaned close to absorb every precious word. A second later, she was jolted from her hero worship by Bell's elbow.

"We have to go," Bell whispered. "Now!"

The detectives quietly exited the courtroom and walked down the hallway to the stairs. Nicole was trying to keep up with Bell, who was approaching a near sprint.

"John!" She started after him. "What is it? What's the matter?"

Bell threw open the stairwell door, took a few steps, and turned to Nicole on the stairway landing.

"I cannot believe I've been so freakin' stupid!" he yelled.

"What? John, what are you talking about?" Nicole asked.

"Emma! The call, Nicole," Bell replied. "She said something about Durkin hiring under the table."

Nicole scrunched up her brow in confusion, still unable to make the connection, or to determine why Bell thought himself stupid.

"Okay…"

"Sorry," Bell said. "A day or two after Kevin Myers was murdered, I received a call from a woman claiming that Durkin pays people under the table to work at the restaurant. I didn't think much of it, because…well, why would I? I'm sure it happens all the time, and it's not really my problem, right?"

"Right. So…?" Nicole asked.

"So, Emma calls today and tells me that Daryl and Lawrence didn't show up for work and Durkin is super pissed. Then she repeats the same rumor the caller told me, about him hiring under the table. She even mentioned the IRS, for God's sake, like she was trying to pound home the point. This is the second time I've gotten a call about it, and both times the caller's been a female."

"Do you think it was Emma the first time?" Nicole asked.

"I don't know, and I can't remember what the first woman sounded like," Bell admitted. "Either way, I'm not comfortable writing it off to coincidence.

I think we should at least look into Mr. Durkin's hiring practices. I also think we should take another look at Emma. If she is the same woman who called the first time, I want to know why she's got such a hard-on for this angle, for exposing her boss's illicit activities."

"Okay," Nicole said. "Where to?"

"For now," Bell replied, "let's get back to Homicide and fill Baker in."

A short while later, they were walking into Baker's office. They'd decided beforehand that Nicole do the talking and tell the sergeant about their still-forming theory, as she got along with him much better than Bell did.

Baker hunched over some paperwork, seated behind his desk, a beat-up wooden contraption that was far beyond seeing its better days. Decoration was sparse: There were a few photos of Baker's wife and children on the desk and on the bookcase behind him, which was spilling over with books about forensics, profiling, and other modern policing techniques. The window was so filthy that there might as well not have been one at all; light could barely make its way through the dingy glass.

Baker looked up as they entered.

"What do you two want?" he grunted.

"It's about the Myers case, sir." Nicole took a step closer and briefly outlined the new information about the under the table employee angle.

"So? Sounds like an IRS or INS problem to me."

"Sir, if the two calls are connected, then the murder itself might be connected. Was Kevin Myers murdered because he was going to report Durkin for illegal hiring practices? If so, sir, this could blow the case wide open."

"Hmm. Well, sounds to me like you're a bit long on speculation and short on facts."

"We understand that, sir, but we really feel we'd be amiss if we didn't at least investigate this angle. We don't want to leave any stone unturned. If there's nothing to it, we won't be any worse off."

"Fine," Baker snapped, slamming his pen down. "Investigate if you must, but don't do a damn thing that'll piss off the wrong people. Capiche?"

"Yes, sir. Thank you." Nicole herded Bell out before he could say anything the two of them would regret, closing the door behind them.

Bell ran a hand through his short black hair, a move Nicole recognized as his mantra of frustration. "What a rousing endorsement," he groused.

"Look, just be grateful he didn't put the kibosh on it."

"You're right, as usual." Bell smiled. Nicole looked especially good that morning, dressed in a classic pair of black slacks paired with a pale green blouse that emphasized her fair skin and ash-blonde hair. Her face was a bit more wan than usual, but Bell marked that down to the pressures of the case. *Damn, That Jeff Ellis is one lucky bastard.*

They sat down at their desks to put their heads together.

"We need a game plan. Not only do we need to check out the hiring thing, but we've also got to talk to Mrs. Durkin about her story and send someone back to the strip club to find out more about Durkin's visits there."

"Why don't you head down to Durkin's to talk to Emma? I think she likes you," Nicole teased, then continued before Bell could come up with a retort. "I'll talk to Mrs. Durkin, and we can send either Brian Karpinsky or Bill King back to Dalia's to follow up with…uh, what was her name? Diamond? Bambi? Lambchop?"

Bell smiled and flipped through his notebook. "Jenna – or at least that's her stage name. Apparently Durkin has a thing for her." He looked at his watch and saw that it was close to noon. "Jenna doesn't work until later tonight, so I can go back with Karpinsky. He went with me the first time. Let's split up. We can meet back here and then grab a late lunch."

"Don't you want to eat at Durkin's?" Nicole's eyes twinkled.

"You know, I do have a cast-iron stomach, but I'm not in the mood for greasy spoon food today." He watched Nicole leave, then wandered over to the other side of the room, where Karpinsky was on the phone. When he hung up, Bell asked if Karpinsky could ride take a trip out to Dalia's later.

"Let's see. So you're asking me if I'd rather sit here pushing paper around on my desk of visit a club full of scantily clad working girls? Hmm. Let me think about it for a minute…"

"Funny, Karpinsky." After receiving the curt affirmative, Bell left the building and made his way through the congested city streets to the home of congested arteries, Durkin's Restaurant.

Chapter Ten

Nicole pulled up in front of the Durkin's townhouse on Catharine Street. Just as before, she could hear the television blaring as she approached the entrance. It took several minutes after her ringing the bell for Alice Durkin to answer the door.

Alice seemed surprised, but she invited Nicole to enter.

Alice didn't look quite as put together as she had the last time Nicole and Bell stopped by. While her clothing was just as nice, her hair was frowzy, and she hadn't bothered with makeup, so there was a blatant puffiness under her eyes that Nicole had noticed on her last visit.

They sat down in the properly appointed living room. Nicole glanced around and saw that it was messy, unlike before.

Alice caught her eye and laughed somewhat ruefully.

"Oh, I must apologize for the state of the place. I'm usually quite a neat freak, but I haven't had a chance to straighten up yet." She held her hand up to her mouth and gave a slight hiccough. "Sorry. My breakfast seems to be repeating on me. Now, what is it I can do for you?"

An odd odor that Nicole couldn't quite place reached her nose. Ignoring it for the moment, she smiled at Alice and withdrew her trusty notebook from her pocket. "I promise I won't keep you long, but we just have a few more questions about the night of the murder. You don't mind, do you?"

Alice's eyes widened slightly. "Of course not." She leaned in toward Nicole. "Are you any closer to finding the murderer?"

"We're working on a number of leads," Nicole replied, careful as always not to let any unnecessary information slip. She noticed that the odor was stronger when Alice shifted position. Looking down at her notes, she continued, "You told my partner and me that last Friday night, you were watching television and your husband arrived home at 11:30. Is that correct?"

"Yes, that's correct." Her hands were folded in her lap.

"You're sure about that?"

"Yes, I'm sure." Her voice took on a harder note. "Why do you ask?"

"It's just that we've received some new information." Nicole paused, watching Alice's face carefully.

Alice blinked. "New information?"

"Apparently, one of the employees at the restaurant heard you and your husband talking in the office this morning." Alice's knuckles started to turn white. "You were overheard saying that you didn't remember, and your husband was telling you to stick to your story. Would you care to comment?"

A moment of silence followed, punctuated only by the nattering of the women on *The View* coming from the flat-screen television in the corner. Nicole kept her eyes on the woman sitting across from her, who didn't seem to know which way to look. Finally Alice's face crumpled.

"It's true." Wiping her eyes, Alice continued with a tremor in her voice. "I don't remember what happened that night. I wasn't watching television. I had been, but I'd conked out on the couch some time after 9:00. I always fall asleep early, and when Reggie gets home, if I've fallen asleep in here, he drags me to bed."

"So you don't remember what time he got home?"

"No. I was in no condition to remember anything." Tears continued to pour down her face. "See...Well, I have a problem."

Realization hit Nicole: Alice's puffy eyes, the somewhat unpleasant odor and the well-stocked bar in the corner of the living room all began to make sense.

"You were *passed out* that night and can't remember when your husband arrived?"

"Yes." Sensing a sympathetic ear, Alice rushed on. "Reggie is away so much, between his work and his nights out at Dalia's." At Nicole's start of surprise, Alice laughed bitterly. "Oh, he thinks I don't know about his frequent visits to that strip joint, but I'm well aware. How could I not know when my so-called friends make sure to fill me in on all the gory details because they're 'concerned' about my welfare? It's hard spending night after night at home, with only the television and a cat for company. We have no children. We were unable to have them, and Reggie refused to adopt. When the restaurant started to stabilize after the first few years, he told me no wife of his was going to work there – or anywhere. He didn't want anyone to think we were needy or unsuccessful."

Nicole felt a rush of pity. She had an aunt who was an alcoholic, and like Mrs. Durkin, her problem had been fed in part by an absentee husband. For years she'd been in denial about her condition. Yet she had a job to do, and she knew she had to keep her natural impulse to offer help in check. "Did your husband tell you where he was?"

"I knew he was supposed to close that night, so I figured that was where he was, unless he went to Dalia's afterward. It was only after we found out about the murder that he told me I had to tell you when he got home. He even checked the *TV Guide* to see what aired that night so we could make the story sound authentic." She began sobbing harder.

"Is there anything else you haven't told us?"

"No. That's it. I was just so ashamed about my problem, and of course, I don't want my husband to get into trouble. He couldn't have done such a horrible thing. He may not be the best husband in the world, but he's a decent man. He said he got home at 11:30 and just needed me to verify his story. I wouldn't have lied if I didn't believe it."

Nicole rose, snapping her notebook shut. "Thank you, Mrs. Durkin. I'll see myself out."

Alice, still seated, clutched at the hem of Nicole's jacket. "What's going to happen now? Will he be...arrested?"

"If your husband can produce another alibi, he has nothing to worry about."

Nicole gently disengaged herself from the distraught woman and left her sitting in a heap on the couch. Getting into her car, she headed to her rendezvous with Bell at headquarters.

While Nicole was hearing Alice Durkin's confession, Bell was sitting in his car, parked a few hundred yards from the entrance to Durkin's Restaurant. He pulled out his cell and dialed the restaurant number. As he waited to speak to Emma, he idly watched the pedestrians on the sidewalk, taking advantage of a sunny early spring day. Mothers pushed babies in strollers, and several older couples walked by, some holding hands. He thought of his own parents, who had been married nearly forty years; he couldn't imagine them holding hands or even taking a leisurely stroll down the street. His mother was always too busy with her clubs and committees, and his father seemed to enjoy playing handyman around the house, especially since he was retired.

"Hello, Emma? Yeah, hi. It's me, Detective Bell. Listen, I'd like to talk to you but I'd rather meet somewhere other than the restaurant. Do you have a break anytime soon?" He looked at his watch. "Yes, I can wait. I'm parked down the street, right in front of the hardware store."

He turned off his phone and leaned back on the seat, idly wondering what Renee was up to with her ad agency boyfriend. He chuckled at the thought of her being in a relationship with the kind of guy who could have walked right off the set of *Mad Men*, the kind of guy who'd fit right in in a culture where men were men and the women just fetched the coffee while looking fetching. He nearly jumped out of his seat when a knock came on his window.

There was Emma, wearing a bulky gray cardigan, her apron flapping in the breeze.

Bell rolled down the window. "Hop in. I won't keep you long. I know you have to get back to work."

She made her way around to the passenger side of the car and slid into the seat. Her cheeks were pink, and it certainly wasn't just because of the nip in the air.

"Thanks for the call this morning," Bell began.

"Yeah, well, I hope I didn't do the wrong thing. I wasn't sure if the information would be useful, and I kind of feel like a tattletale."

"Well, it's part of my job to sift through it all to find the useful information and toss out the junk." He smiled at her, and her cheeks went from pink to red. "It's kind of like sorting the mail."

"So, um, what is it you need? I only have about ten minutes."

"Right, sorry. I just wanted to follow up with you on the illegal alien thing."

"What?"

"You said this morning that Daryl and Lawrence hadn't come to work."

"Right."

"You also mentioned rumors about your boss's illegal hiring practices."

"Yeah, but I thought we went over all of this on the phone."

"Well, when we first began to investigate this case, we received an anonymous call from a woman who told us she believed Kevin might have been killed because Durkin hires guys under the table, and Kevin might have known too much."

There was a long pause.

"Was that you?"

Another pause, and Emma bit her bottom lip.

"Well?" Bell prompted again.

Emma sighed. "Yes, that was me. I was just trying to help, really."

"What proof do you have of any of this?"

"None, really. It's just that…" She exhaled sharply. "It just really cheeses me off that Durkin gets away with being a cheapskate, paying people probably far less than what they're worth by doing things illegally."

Bell frowned slightly. This information was not good news for his recent hypothesis. "Did you ever think of reporting him yourself?"

"And lose my job? Listen, I wanted to go to cosmetology school after high school, but I couldn't afford it. I know it's just waitressing and nothing glamorous like you do, but right now, this job's all I've got." She looked away.

"I figured maybe if I tipped you off during a murder investigation, something would be done about it, that's all."

"You do realize you wasted our time with that tip?"

"I'm sorry." Emma trembled in the seat next to him. "I guess I didn't think about that. Still…" She faltered slightly.

"Yes?" Bell tried to keep the impatience out of his voice.

"It's just that the timing of Lawrence's and Daryl's disappearance is pretty coincidental. I mean, they were pretty good workers and seemed to like their jobs well enough. Why would they just take off so suddenly?"

She had a point, but if it turned out the two men had anything to do with Kevin Myers's murder, Bell didn't want to speculate further with a potential witness. He smiled. "I'd better let you get back to work."

"You're not mad?"

"No, I'm not mad - well, maybe just a little. But I understand where you're coming from. Next time, though, just think before you do something like that."

"I hope there isn't a next time. This has been one of the most miserable weeks of my life." She grasped the door handle and then turned back. "Do you know when the funeral is? I'd like to pay my respects."

"I don't know. I'll let you know as soon as I find out."

Later, when Bell and Nicole met up at Homicide HQ and exchanged stories, Nicole was slightly stunned at Bell's news. "So that puts us right back at square one."

"Not necessarily." Bell tapped his pencil lightly on the desktop. "Emma's right about one thing."

"What's that?"

"It's pretty fishy that those two hot-footed it during our investigation. Myers was apparently their friend. Friends sometimes argue, though, and arguments can escalate into violence, especially among guys."

"And especially when drugs or alcohol are involved."

"His toxicology report came back clean."

"Yeah, but who knows what state his two pals were in?" Nicole countered.

"Good point. But what about Durkin? Now that his alibi has fallen apart, we'll have to talk to him again."

"I suppose, but let's have lunch first. Then we can figure out our next step."

"Let's do Geno's."

"Oh, please not cheesesteak. It's so fattening."

"Your choice next time. Promise."

She sighed. "Okay, you win." *Besides,* she thought, *temporary weight gain will soon be the least of her problems. Hey, when do I get to start using that 'I'm eating for two now' excuse?*

As the two detectives sat on a bench finishing their sandwiches, Bell received a call.

Nicole watched his face turn pale as he listened to the person on the other end.

"Okay," he said gruffly. "Thanks for telling me." He looked at what was left of his cheesesteak, wadded it in the paper wrapper, and tossed it into a nearby garbage can.

"What is it?" Nicole asked with some trepidation.

"Damn!" Bell shouted.

"What is it?!" she shouted back.

Bell's breath was coming out in short bursts through his nose. "That…that fucking bastard!"

"Who?"

"Drew Nichols."

Nicole waited for the rest.

"Apparently, he spent his evening beating Ellie Jacobson into a pulp. She's in the ICU. They don't know if she's going to make it."

The blood drained out of Nicole's face. "That sweet little thing? My God. Why?"

"No idea, but he's back in custody."

"Well, I guess that means we've got ourselves a change in plans, huh?"

"You bet. Let's go," Bell said grimly.

Bell and Nicole walked into Divisional Headquarters at Harbison and Levick Streets. The building was shared between the detectives (who occupied the second floor) and the 15th and 2nd Police Districts (both on the first floor). They headed upstairs, where Divisional Detective Billy Flynn was waiting. A former Army sergeant, Flynn was also a combat vet, having done a tour during the first Gulf War. After his honorable discharge, he went to college on the GI bill, where he studied criminal justice and afterward joined the force. He wasn't the tallest guy in the room, but he stood out. He had a perpetual twinkle in his eye and was a general favorite amongst his co-workers.

"Hi, Billy. Thanks for calling us in." Bell gripped Flynn's hand.

"No problem. The doer says he's already been grilled by you two about a homicide, so I thought I'd invite you to sit in on this session in case anything relevant comes up." He handed them the report written by the officers who had responded to the 911 call.

Nicole held the report while Bell read it over her shoulder. Apparently, Drew had forced his way into Ellie Jacobson's home and beaten the old woman so badly that her face was almost unrecognizable and her brain was swelling. She had also suffered some cracked ribs. Nicole blinked hard.

"Who called it in?"

"The neighbors in the next house over. Apparently, he was yelling so loud that they could hear it from over there."

Nicole looked up at Bell. She couldn't read his face. She handed the report back to Billy, her hand shaking slightly, and the two of them followed him down the hall.

They walked into the interview room, which was almost identical to the one in Homicide – a dreary, cinderblock room painted a nauseating green with a table in the center.

Drew Nichols was already seated in the chair that was bolted down to the floor, his left hand locked in the handcuffs attached to the chair.

"Shit," he murmured when Bell and Nicole entered. Although he'd had a few fantasies about the blonde since the last time he'd seen her, she and the bastard with her were the last people he wanted to see in that moment.

"Hey Drew," Bell said slowly and deliberately. "Long time, no see." Nicole half-expected her partner to grab Nichols and throw him around the room, but Bell's self-control got the better of him. Neither detective wanted to jeopardize the case or infringe upon Billy Flynn's investigation, so they tried to keep quiet and observe. Their mere presence was intimidating enough.

Flynn sat down across from Nichols, while Bell and Nicole stood. All three detectives had the feeling that Drew would lawyer up and that the interview would not be a lengthy one.

"Good afternoon, Mr. Nichols," Flynn began. "I am Detective Flynn of Northeast Detective Division. I believe you already know Detectives Bell and Ellis."

"Yeah," Nichols responded.

"Well, Mr. Nichols, I have some good news and some bad news. The bad news is that you are facing a barrelful of charges - attempted murder, aggravated assault, simple assault, burglary, reckless endangerment, terroristic threats, and unlawful restraint. The good news is that you have a chance to help yourself today by talking to us. You tell us your side of the story, and the jury will know that you were at least cooperative."

Drew Nichols stared at Flynn, stone-faced. He didn't say a word.

Flynn continued. "Look, Drew, we are not going to sit here and waste everyone's time. If you are going to talk to us, fine. If not, we'll take you back downstairs to your cell, and the judge and jury will be told that you refused to cooperate. It's your choice."

"Yeah," Drew mumbled. "My choice? Right. Fine, let's do this, but you'd better read me my rights first."

Bell rolled his eyes at Nicole and thought to himself, *This tool has had his rights read to him so often that he knows them by heart.* Even veteran detectives read them from a sample card or straight from the interview/interrogation Form 75-331; it was one way to ensure that no mistakes would be made that might let a criminal loose on a technicality.

Flynn pulled up the 75-331 on his computer and began reading Nichols his rights. When he was finished, Flynn fired the first salvo.

"Okay, Drew, here's what we know. At approximately 12:30 p.m. today, someone kicked in the rear door of Ellie Jacobson's residence. Soon afterward, witnesses heard you inside the residence, screaming at the top of your lungs. The witnesses called 911, and when the 15th District officers arrived, they found you in the home and Mrs. Jacobson beaten within an inch of her life. Oh yeah, I almost forgot...your clothes were spattered with blood – the victim's blood."

If anything Flynn said affected Drew Nichols, it did not show. The man continued to stare at Flynn, stone-faced.

"That sure is a hell of a lot of evidence against you, Drew," Flynn said. "Maybe you would like to explain yourself?"

Nichols smirked and shrugged his shoulders. "Nothing to explain, Detective. I didn't touch the old broad."

"Really?" Flynn asked. "That's what you're going with? You must think we're stupid."

"Yes...and yes," Drew responded. "But it doesn't matter what I think about you, because this time I didn't do nothin' and you can't prove I did."

Behind Flynn, Bell just shook his head. It was okay that Drew Nichols was a moron, but it bothered Bell when people assumed him to be of the same pathetic ilk. Bell remained steadfast, although the urge to take over the interrogation and return the beating-to-a-pulp favor to Drew was getting stronger. He was chomping at the bit to rake Nichols over the coals, but he knew that time would come soon enough. For his part, Billy Flynn was doing a terrific job.

"Okay, Drew," Flynn began, "now how about you tell me what happened?"

"No problem," Nichols replied. "I heard the old bag screaming like a banshee. I thought maybe she was having a heart attack or fell and broke her hip like those old hags in the bathtub commercials, so I rushed over to see if I could help. The front door was locked tight, and Jacobson always keeps her curtains closed so no one can look in and see her 200 cats. I checked out the back and saw that the door was busted in. I went inside to check on her, and found her on the floor. She was a bloody mess. I didn't know what to do. So I tried to do CPR, and I got her blood all over my shirt. Before I could call 911, the cops showed up, threw the cuffs on me, and dragged me here. And that was all she wrote."

Bell and Nicole looked at each other, their mouths agape. *Does this idiot really expect anyone to believe this nonsense?* Bell wondered, knowing by her facial expression that Nicole was wondering the same thing.

Curiously enough, Flynn was thinking the exact thing.

"Okay, Drew," he said. "Let's try to clarify your statement for the record, okay?"

"Sure. It's all good, man," Drew replied.

While the crime scene had not yet been fully processed, Detective Flynn had been briefed by the detective on the scene. Billy was the assigned, but Northeast Detective Division, like many divisions in the city, had its own crime scene detective. In this case that was Detective Chris Junod, a man so good at his craft that he could probably pull fingerprints from a slab of concrete. Chris called before the interview and said there was plenty of evidence at the scene, though there was nothing that pointed directly at Drew. "Well, not yet," he'd said. "Of course, that may change once the DNA evidence is processed."

"I want to make sure I have your statement correct, Drew, so you will need to indulge me for a minute," Flynn explained. "Let's look at your statement line by line and clear up any questions. You said you heard Ellie Jacobson screaming. Where were you when you first heard her?"

"What?" Drew asked.

Nicole couldn't stifle her smile because she knew that when a suspect asks a detective to repeat the question, he is usually stalling for time – at least enough time to think of a good lie. Responding to a question with "What?" is a variation on a theme. Nichols was lying: Bell knew it. Nicole knew it, Billy Flynn knew it, and Drew Nichols knew it.

Flynn repeated the question. "I asked where you were when you first heard Ellie Jacobson screaming."

"Oh," Nichols replied. "I was on my front step."

"You were on your front step and you heard an old woman screaming, uh…from inside her house? While her windows and doors were closed? Is that your story?" Flynn asked, making it sound as ridiculous as it was.

"Well, yeah," Nichols replied.

"Okay," Flynn said. "You said you heard Ellie screaming and you thought she was having a heart attack or broke her hip or something, so you rushed over to her house to see if you could help her. Is that correct?"

Drew smiled. "Yep."

"Wow. You're just a whore with a heart of gold, aren't you?" Flynn asked.

Drew smirked. "Maybe."

"Let me ask you this then. If you thought Ellie was having a heart attack or something, why didn't you just call 911 instead of taking the time to rush over to her house, especially since you have never gotten along with her?"

"Call an ambulance? In this city?" Nichols asked. "With the mayor's fire department cutbacks, an ambulance would have taken a year to get there. I figured she's as old as Yoda, anyway. She didn't have that kind of time."

"Well, that," Bell interjected, "and if you dialed 911, they might've arrived while you were beating the hell out of Ellie. You couldn't have that now, could you?"

Nicole shot Bell a look, but Flynn did not turn around. If Bell's outburst bothered him, he didn't show it.

Nichols looked up at Bell. "Nice try, Bell, but that's bullshit."

Flynn continued. "You said Ellie didn't have that kind of time, but I'm curious about something."

"What's that?"

"If she didn't have that kind of time, like you said, why did you bother going around to check the back door? Why not just burst in and save her?"

"Right," Drew spat. "And have ten people tell the cops that they saw me breaking into an old woman's house? No thanks. I could do without a burglary pinch."

While it pained him to think that way, Bell had to admit that Nichols was holding his own. Drew was guilty as sin – maybe guiltier – but, he was making the detectives work for their money.

"So you hear the screams, run over to the house, check the doors, and find the back door kicked in. Is that right?"

"Yeah, pretty much," Drew responded. "I don't know if the door was kicked in or pushed in or whatever, but it was open."

"Okay. So then what did you see?" Flynn asked.

"I saw some blood in the kitchen, and it led from the back of the house to the front," Drew said. "The chick was at the end of the trail, and man was she fucked up. If you ask me, the old bag musta have pissed off the wrong person."

That last sentence was meant for Bell and Nicole. Drew wanted to get in his jabs, and for the most part, they were landing. Both detectives were becoming very angry.

"What else did you see in the house? Did you see anything that might have served as a weapon?" Flynn asked.

"I couldn't tell," Nichols replied. "The house was a mess, and shit was thrown all over the place. There was a broken lamp near her body, but who knows if that's what she was beaten with? I sure don't." Again, Nichols punctuated his statement with a smirk toward Bell.

Billy deliberately refused to ask about Nichols's claim that he performed CPR; he would play that card later.

"Drew, let me ask you this. How long would you say you were in the house before the police officers arrived?"

Nichols thought for a moment. "Oh, I don't know. About five minutes tops?"

"Are you asking me or telling me?" Flynn asked.

"Just cooperating, Officer," Drew said snidely. "It was no more than five minutes, but I wasn't exactly keeping track of time."

"Good enough. Do you have anything more to add here?"

"No, not really," Drew admitted. "Well, except I hope you guys catch the person who did this. It's a shame what's happened to this town. People aren't even safe in their own homes anymore."

"Okay," Flynn said. "I am going to print this up and let you check it over for errors. When you're finished, I want you to sign and date the bottom of every page. Got it?"

"Sure," Drew responded.

"You are literate, right? You know how to read and write?"

"Funny."

"Good. Make sure you check it for errors. If anything is incorrect here, let me know, and we'll change it. If there is anything I missed, let me know, okay, Drew?"

"Yeah, whatever."

As Nichols started to read the statement, Flynn asked another detective to keep an eye on him.

Flynn, Bell, and Nicole excused themselves and stepped out of the room.

"Well, what do you think?" Flynn asked.

"I think I want to strangle this asshole, Billy," Bell replied. "He beat the shit out of her, and he's basically laughing about it and giving us the damn finger."

"I know," Flynn said. "Chris is processing the scene now, and he's as good as any CSU tech in the department. He told me there is a lot of evidence there, so there's a good chance we'll be able to clear this case quickly. I would love to see this toad pinched today, but I would also like to see Ellie Jacobson make it through."

"Billy," Nicole began, "I'm not trying to nitpick, but there's a reason you didn't ask him about his attempted CPR, right?"

"Yeah," Flynn replied. "I am hoping he signs and dates the interview without mentioning it. If so, I'll go after him from that angle and see if he breaks. It's a long shot, but this guy had an answer for everything today. It's complete shenanigans, but he's not breaking like I thought he would. There's no way in hell he's been through any CPR training, though I'm sure he's sucked face with a lot of dummies in his day."

Nicole laughed. "Right. I was hoping that was where you were going."

"Hey, just because they keep rejecting my application to Homicide doesn't mean I'm completely stupid." Flynn laughed.

The three detectives walked back into the interview room and saw Drew sitting straight, his hands folded on top of the signed statement. The pose reminded Flynn of his sixteen years of Catholic education, but it wasn't long before he surmised that Nichols was no angel. *The kid would probably catch fire if he set foot inside a church.*

"How we doing, Drew?" Flynn asked. "Did you read everything over?"

"Yep," Nichols replied. "It's all good, man. No mistakes."

"You're sure?" Flynn asked.

"Sure I'm sure."

Flynn took the statement and reread it for Nichols's benefit. He already knew the question that was about to be asked, but he figured he'd let Nichols stew for a minute or two.

"Hmm," Flynn half-whispered.

"What?" Nichols asked.

"Are you sure you can read?"

"Huh? Why are you askin' me that?"

"Well, because in your original statement, you said that after you entered Jacobson's house, you saw her 'bloody mess' and tried to perform CPR. Is that correct?"

Drew swallowed hard. "Uh…what?"

"What?" Flynn repeated. "Is that what you said? Should I speak up, Drew? You said you tried to perform CPR and that was how you got her blood on your shirt. You do remember saying that, right? Because you read and signed the interview stating just that."

"Um, yeah," Drew stuttered. "Yeah, I tried to perform CPR, and my shirt got all bloody. Why?'"

"Okay," Flynn continued. "Let me ask you this. If you tried to perform CPR, why didn't you have blood on your mouth when the officers brought you in? Why isn't there any on your mouth now? Did you have time to stop at the powder room during your arrest?"

Again, Drew swallowed and repeated, "What?"

"Your mouth." Flynn demanded. "Why isn't there any blood on your mouth and face? If you really tried to perform CPR, you would have done chest compressions and rescue breathing. You can't give someone breaths if you don't make contact with their face, Drew - or were you stoned that day of class and forgot that part? Maybe you tried to perform rescue breathing through her ears?"

"Um, no…I-" Drew stammered.

Flynn quickly stood up, forcing his chair to fall over on the floor. Bell, Nicole and Drew jumped a little at the quick movement.

"You're a liar, Nichols!" Flynn screamed. "You forced your way into Ellie Jacobson's house and beat that poor woman half to death like some kind of psychopathic thug! I know it, and you know it!"

Drew Nichols was visibly shaken, but just when he thought Flynn was going to hit him, the detective stopped, changed his tone of voice, and calmly resumed speaking.

"The second the crime scene is processed, we're going to have you dead to rights. There is a bloody footprint in the living room that we are going to match to your sneakers. There are bound to be fingerprints on the lamp and the door, not to mention hair fibers. It's called DNA, Drew, and it is going to seal your fate. The gun and drug charges you're already facing will feel like a vacation compared to this. With your record, an attempted murder charge will keep you holed up in Graterford for a long, long time – and boy are your cellies gonna like the sight of your scrawny little ass."

Drew Nichols said nothing, but his body language was talking nonstop. He was scared, and the smirk he'd so cockily displayed only minutes earlier was replaced with darting eyes and quivering lips.

Just when he thought it couldn't get any worse, the door opened, and in marched Flynn's supervisor, Lieutenant Stephen Coles.

"Billy, can I talk to you guys for a second?" he asked.

"Sure, Lieutenant." Flynn responded. Billy left the room with Bell and Nicole in tow.

"What's up, boss?" Flynn asked.

"Ellie Jacobson was just pronounced. Forget the assault. It's now a homicide."

"Jesus Christ," Bell muttered.

Flynn made the Sign of the Cross and shook his head. "Okay, boss. We'll get a wagon in here to transport him to Homicide. Bell, do you want me to call the CSU to process the scene?"

"No. If Junod is as thorough as you say he is, I have no problem with him finishing up," Bell replied. "Nic, are you okay with that?"

"Sure," Nicole replied. "Thanks, Billy."

"No problem," Flynn responded. "Do you want me to tell him the good news, or do you guys want to do it?"

"Still your case, Billy. Feel free," Bell said, even though he would have loved to break the news to Drew himself.

The detectives entered the interrogation room.

Nichols lifted his head up from the table. He did not like the looks on their faces.

"Ellie Jacobson is dead, Drew," Flynn said matter-of-factly. "You are going to be charged with her murder."

After all of his bluster, all of his bragging, Drew Nichols' tough-guy attitude finally cracked. The drug-dealing, gun-toting skinhead started to sniffle, and then he openly wept.

"Not smiling now, are you, scumbag?" Bell asked before leaving the room, ironically wearing a big grin of his own.

Chapter Eleven

That Tuesday evening, Detective Brian Karpinsky entered Dalia's Delights to speak to Jenna, as asked. Usually he disliked playing second fiddle on a case, but in this instance, it gave him the chance to rub elbows with the tasty Nicole Ellis, who very rarely partnered with anyone but John Bell.

Like Bell, he found Nicole attractive; unlike Bell, however, he wouldn't have minded acting upon that attraction. He wasn't all that opposed to being a home-wrecker, because he didn't really care about his own home life. His own wife hadn't aged well, and their marriage had soured years ago. His colleagues' suspicions about that were correct, but they were incorrect about the reason why he wouldn't divorce; it had less to do with religion and more to do with the fact that he knew his vindictive wife would take him to the cleaners. Karpinsky enjoyed his creature comforts. A little T&A on the side kept him satisfied, and years of training his expressions as a detective – and the fact that he was often out at all hours on the job - helped keep the comparative peace at home.

What he wouldn't have given for a fling with Nicole! That sap, Bill King, was nice to her because he really did believe in equality of the sexes on the job, but Brian's motives had more to do with his secret desire than anything that smacked of Title IX. He knew she was devoted to her husband, but he was keenly aware that police marriages have a habit of breaking down; after all, his own was nothing to mention. He decided that when things fell apart for Nicole when Jeff decided to hit the highway, he'd be there to help her pick up the pieces.

In the meantime, he had a job to do. As a rule, Brian didn't mind strip clubs. In fact, he occasionally frequented a few upscale ones on his time off, careful not to spend too much time at any one in particular. However, Dalia's wasn't up to his high standards. Old and dank, with clientele who bordered on skanky, it was not a building Brian would enter on other than official business.

As he approached the bar, Vic the bartender recognized him and waved him over.

"You're one of those guys from Homicide, right?"

"That's right."

"Here to see Jenna?"

"If she's here."

"She's in the back, getting ready. Wanna head back there?"

"If it's not inconvenient," Karpinsky answered, a bit more eager than he should have been to have a backstage pass at a strip club.

"Sure. Right through there." Vic pointed to a door to the side of the bar. Thanking him, Brian walked through it and easily found what passed for a dressing room. There were a few scantily clad women in there, but only one seemed like she could be Jenna. Seated at a makeup table with a mirror sporting glaring light bulbs, her golden blonde hair piled high on her head and clad only in a sequined purple push-up bra and matching G-string, she was applying a deep red lipstick to her full lips. She was magnificent. *Damn. Too bad I'm here on official business,* Brian thought when she turned to face him.

"Jenna?" Brian inquired.

"Who let you back here? Employees only," she snapped.

The other two women simply stared at him as if he had – or was – a disease.

Brian held out his ID. "Detective Brian Karpinsky, Homicide, Philly PD," he said quickly to dispel any fears she might have.

Her face softened a bit. "Oh, right. Vic told me you might be by sometime. Have a seat." She patted a stool next to her. "I have a few minutes." She turned back to the mirror as Brian approached and sat down as instructed. A closer view showed that under all of her makeup, Jenna was probably barely over twenty years old, and he thought it sad that she likely wouldn't keep her looks long in her line of work.

"What's this all about?" she asked as she applied a pencil marked "Chocolate Sin" to her eyebrows.

"Reginald Durkin. Do you know him?"

"Reggie? Know him? If I knew him any better, we'd be married." She laughed. "Well, not really, but he's in here a lot. He only comes to see me," she said, sounding like a flattered schoolgirl.

"Do you remember him coming in with this man?" Brian showed her Kevin Myers's picture.

She leaned over to look at it, affording Brian a direct view of her overly large breasts. She sat in quiet thought for a few moments.

"Yeah. Yeah, I remember him. Nice guy, kind of quiet and polite. You don't get much of that around here. I had the feeling he was a little uncomfortable, but Reggie brought him in for his birthday. I guess he wanted to show him a good time. Wait…did you say you were with Homicide? What happened to the poor guy?"

"He was murdered." Brian kept the information to a minimum. While the Myers murder had already been reported in the papers and on the local news, he had the feeling Jenna wasn't one for keeping an eye on current events, and he didn't want to plant any information in her mind that wasn't already there.

"Gee, that's too bad." She didn't look terribly upset, but then, Brian reasoned, she didn't really know the guy - at least not that he knew.

"Did he get into an argument with anyone here? Did anyone give him a hard time?"

"There were a few looks when he came in." Her voice lowered to a whisper, as if she feared offending anyone within earshot. "Um, see, we don't usually get black guys in here. Still, no one bothered him as far as I can recall." She fiddled with her false eyelashes.

"You're sure about that?" Brian pressed further.

She turned and gave him a baleful look. "Yeah, I'm sure. He came, he saw, he shoved a few dollars in my undies, and he went home. Look, if you don't have any other questions, I'm going on in a few, and I need to finish getting ready."

Brian sighed, realizing he'd hit a bit of a wall with the lead. "I guess not." He rose. "Expecting your 'husband' tonight?"

Jenna looked confused for a moment, then laughed. "Who, Reggie? I wouldn't be surprised. He's my best customer."

"Really?" Brian asked, slightly bored now as he turned toward the door.

"Oh yeah. He's a big spender. He loves my private lap dances. I'd say he drops at least a few hundred a week."

Brian stopped suddenly. A few hundred dollars a week for a guy like Reginald Durkin was nothing to sneeze at. "How long has he been coming here?"

"A couple years. He started showing up shortly after I started dancing. You know, I'm gonna be a star someday," she confided. "This is just a temporary gig. I'm gonna be just like Britney Spears. Reggie told me he has connections."

Just then, one of the goons from out front stuck his head through the door frame. "Jenna, you're on," he grunted, giving Brian a dirty look.

Jenna swept by Brian, enveloping him in a cloud of musk.

"Maybe I'll see you around," she purred, patting his behind with a well-manicured hand.

Brian quickly made his way to the front entrance as Jenna began gyrating slowly onstage for the appreciative men in the audience, whose numbers had grown since Brian had first arrived. He wasn't sure what it meant, but his cop instinct was in overdrive at the thought that a guy who owned a struggling greasy spoon, with a wife who enjoyed a fairly high standard of living, could afford to spend hundreds of dollars a week on private lap dances from the likes of Jenna. *Could he be getting his money illegally? Perhaps embezzling it from the business? Did Kevin Myers know something about it? Did he end up paying for that knowledge with his life?* Brian hopped into his car, but before starting his engine, he took out his cell phone and punched in Bell's number.

"So what do you think it means?" Nicole asked Bell. Her stomach gave a sudden lurch, and she fought hard to keep Bell from noticing that anything was wrong.

Bell wouldn't have noticed a nuclear attack, though, for he was too deep in thought, and her momentary discomfort wasn't going to make a dent.

"Maybe it's like Brian said. Maybe he was cooking the books and Kevin found out."

"Maybe."

"What the hell did Jenna mean about Reggie having connections that would help her become a big celebrity?"

"Please," Nicole snorted. "You've seen – and smelled – the guy, right? What else could he possibly say to keep her interested?"

"Girls like her are interested in only one thing, and it's green."

"Yes, but if he wanted her to be interested in more than just his money, he'd have to impress her somehow, and I doubt his looks are enough."

Bell scratched his forehead just above his eyebrow. "This isn't getting us anywhere. We need a warrant to search his personal and business financial records."

"Well? What are we waiting for?" The wave of nausea had passed, and Nicole was eager to dig in to the latest development. She retrieved her personal laptop from her drawer in one of the file cabinets nearby and quickly set it on the desk in front of her.

In order to receive a copy of Durkin's financial records and those of his diner, the detectives would have to obtain a search warrant. In the interim, they could issue a subpoena *duces tecum* to the appropriate entity to secure the documents in a more timely fashion. The *duces tecum* is similar to the search warrant, in that it contains a detailed description of the evidence desired. It does not necessarily require the description of the circumstances that led to the request, however. For example, Nicole would request copies of Durkin's personal and financial statement, but she would not include details of the investigation at hand.

Nicole pulled up a copy of the *duces tecum* on her computer and stood up. "I'll let you take care of this. You're the master, after all. I have a couple personal phone calls to make. Then I'll make the other calls we'll need to make." She took a chair at the next desk and pulled out her cell phone.

Bell stretched out a yawn and stood up. He needed caffeine. There was a soda machine down the hallway, and a brisk walk would be just the thing to get the blood pumping. As he walked in pursuit of a carbonated, caffeinated beverage, he thought about Durkin. *Does that greasy weasel really have the wontons to kill a man? If so, what the hell was the motive here?* Bell was so preoccupied with the questions that he walked right by the machine and found himself standing in front of the men's room.

Bell smiled as he muttered, "It's a sign."

When he was in college, Bell wrote for the university newspaper. He had a knack for writing, and he truly enjoyed it. The fact that he could think of an idea, then sit down and effortlessly pump out 800 words had both pleased and infuriated his fellow writers. When the rare case of writer's block ensnared him, he had a unique way of breaking the curse: a trip to the closest men's room.

In the Campus Activities Building, the restrooms were on the second floor, while the newspaper office was on the third. Whenever Bell was stuck for an idea, he would jog down the stairs, go into the men's room, and approach a urinal. Since he virtually subsisted off Dr. Pepper, he always had to go. By the time he was finished, he had found a solution to his issue. It never failed.

After a while, it became the office joke. Every time he stepped away from his computer, his friends would yell,

"Writer's block!"

In one particularly embarrassing instance, his best friend Dawn had caught him urinating by a tree after he'd had a few too many. Never one to miss an opportunity, Dawn deadpanned, "What's wrong, John? The tree not giving you any newsworthy quotes?"

Bell grinned as he returned to the here and now. Not wanting to tempt fate, or the bathroom gods, he entered the men's room. A minute or so later, he walked out of the room and smiled. While he still did not have answers to the Durkin questions, he did know exactly how he would write the *duces tecum*. Stopping by the soda machine, Bell shook his head at the blinking "Sold Out" on the Dr. Pepper button.

"Oh well." He sighed. "I guess Coke will do in a pinch."

Reentering the squad room, John popped the top and took a gulp of his sugary fuel. He must have been gone longer than he thought, because Nicole had already finished her personal calls and was waiting by the door. She cocked her head and asked, "You okay?"

"Yeah. I was in the bathroom."

"They moved the soda machine into the men's room?" Nicole asked. "Because if that's the case, I'm now a big fan of bottled water."

"No," Bell replied. "It's still in the hallway. I went to the bathroom first – figured I'd save time by taking a preemptive pee, if you must know."

Nicole rolled her eyes and walked away.

Bell shouted, "What?" and shrugged his shoulders.

Her response was a raised hand and a giggle.

Back at his desk, Bell started the *duces tecum*.

Nicole, who had returned to her desk after her giggling fit, made a few calls and found out that Bank of America held the mortgage on Durkin's Restaurant, while the accounting firm of Rosenbaum and Associates kept the books.

Each *duces tecum* would read:

"Request copies of any and all financial paperwork pertaining to Mr. Reginald Durkin and Durkin's Restaurant.

Included in this request are copies of tax returns, pay stubs, and mortgage records from the past three years."

When Bell was working with the divisional detectives, it was common practice to submit a *duces tecum* and forego the search warrant. The businesses and corporations usually complied with the request and rarely demanded further paperwork. The practice was not completely kosher, but it was good enough for their run-of-the-mill fraud cases. Homicide was a different story. Every proverbial i and t had to be proverbially dotted and crossed. If not, even the most incompetent defense attorney could convince a judge to dismiss all charges. As such, Bell and his co-workers ran every investigation by the book. The stakes were simply too high to take shortcuts.

After the *duces tecum* was completed, Bell had Nicole double-check the paperwork for accuracy. Convinced that everything was up to par, Bell faxed it to the pertinent organizations. Nicole called ahead to let the businesses know the subpoenas were coming. When they responded with faxed copies, Bell would then type the search warrants.

Nicole had a question. "Who do you think we should ask to approve the warrants when the time comes?"

Bell sat in silence for a few moments, then snapped his fingers. "Judge Judy," he said, referring to Judge Geraldine Simpson, who held quite a resemblance to the television judge, both physically and temperamentally.

"Think she'll do it?"

"I know she will. Remember the Rodriguez case?"

The Rodriguez case to which Bell was referring was a domestic homicide case in which a successful local businessman, Paul Rodriguez, had bludgeoned his wife to death. It turned out that a paid mistress had been involved, and the financial records Judge Simpson had helped them procure were a big part of their getting an indictment. Rodriguez was later sentenced to twenty to life.

"Great. In the meantime-" Bell's flow of thought was interrupted by the ringing of the phone.

Nicole heard him emit a number of "uh-huhs" and "yeahs," and then he hung up and said, "Someone's on the way up."

"Who?"

"An insurance salesman."

"Is this one of your stupid jokes?"

"No. Jim Roberts is working the front desk, and he said some insurance salesman has some information for us. He's sending him up."

"I've got all the insurance I need at the moment, thanks," Nicole said wryly. She glanced at the door just as a man holding a briefcase was ushered through and was directed toward them. Bell rose to greet him. "Mr. Simmons?"

"Yes. Steve Simmons. Are you Detective Bell?"

"I am, and this is my partner, Detective Ellis."

Simmons's eyes widened slightly when he saw Nicole, a reaction that, Bell reflected, was not unusual for men who were first introduced to his attractive partner.

"Why don't you have a seat?"

Bell indicated an empty chair, and Simmons took it. He looked every inch the proverbial dull insurance salesman, like the one who Bill Murray's character in *Groundhog Day* kept meeting on the street. "How can we help you?"

"Is it too late? I'm sorry I couldn't come by sooner. I only just got off work." He looked around nervously.

"Not to worry, Mr. Simmons," Bell responded. "During a case, we're on the job pretty much around the clock."

"You have some information for us, Mr. Simmons?" Nicole prodded gently. It was true that they sometimes worked around the clock, but she didn't feel like waiting for him to get over what seemed to be the usual nervousness felt by people when they were talking to the cops.

"Yes, yes I do." He withdrew a piece of paper from his briefcase and laid it on the desk, a newspaper clipping about the murder of Kevin Myers, with Kevin's picture prominently displayed. "I'm here about this."

Bell prayed silently that Steve Simmons would not lead them on yet another wild goose chase. "What can you tell us?"

Steve cleared his throat. "I was out of town over the weekend, or else I would have come in sooner." He paused.

"And?" Bell had difficulty keeping his voice calm as his annoyance level grew.

"The thing is, a few months ago, I wrote up a life insurance policy for a Mr. Kevin Myers at the address noted in this article, but the man for whom I wrote the policy looks nothing like the man in this picture."

The two detectives gave each other a long look before Bell turned back to Steve Simmons. "Would you recognize him again if you saw him?"

"Yes, I believe I would."

Bell smiled. "Come with us."

Chapter Twelve

The morning sun broke through the grimy window of the Philadelphia Police SWAT Unit earlier than usual. The days were getting longer, and while that was welcome news for many, the blinding sunlight was not. For Sergeant Anthony "Tony" Capelli, it was yet another grim reminder that the day work tour was in full swing. Tony hated day work for two reasons. First, it meant he had to get up early – 5:00 a.m. to be exact – and he was certainly not a morning person. He consumed the night, and when he was off duty, he could be seen out until the wee hours of the morning drinking, dancing, and making the acquaintance of a lovely lady or two. Of course, that fact led into the second reason why he hated day work: He was sometimes hung over when he walked into the operations room.

Such was the case today, and while the burning sunlight grated upon Capelli's nerves, the ringing telephone sent him into a barely uncontrolled rage. *Who the hell is calling SWAT this early on a Sunday?* he thought. The temptation was there to pick up the receiver and slam it down, but in the end, the sergeant knew the morons would only call back. His throbbing skull couldn't take another series of rings.

"SWAT, Capelli!"

"Yeah, my cat is stuck in a tree, and I was wondering if you could send a team to shoot him down."

"It's far too early for your bullshit, John," replied Tony, "but since I'm in such a good mood today, I won't come down to Homicide beat you to death with your own damn coffee mug. What's hot?"

Bell smiled a little before answering. It was always good to get under the skin of his former partner. "Same crap. Thug kills man. Hero detectives put thug away. Hero detectives get no credit."

A medium-sized athletic man with dark hair and olive skin, Capelli did not look like the stereotypical SWAT team member, and he used that to his advantage against those who underestimated him.

Now it was his turn to laugh. "No credit, but thousands of dollars in overtime. Yeah, you poor baby."

Before Tony's transfer and Bell's promotion, the two had worked a patrol wagon together in the 35th District. Located in the northwestern part of the city, the 35th is always a busy place. They'd appreciated their time there, because after a few years working in that district, one is almost guaranteed to run into every sort of job imaginable. One night they were guarding a homicide scene, and the next night they were breaking up a boisterous college party. Bell preferred the former, while Tony preferred the latter. In fact, he still had a few phone numbers from coeds he'd met at LaSalle University. *Good times*, he recalled fondly as he listened to Bell's voice.

Bell continued, "Hey, Tony, I was wondering if you and your guys could hit a house for me tomorrow. Nicole and I just had an arrest warrant for the doer approved."

Detectives in the Homicide Division made friends fast within the department. Other patrol officers, detectives, and special unit personnel realized that homicide trials were big moneymakers, so they were usually quick to offer their assistance when asked, especially if a court appearance would follow. The Philadelphia Police Department SWAT team was no different. SWAT teams can sometimes be self-serving, but not for monetary reasons. The officers in SWAT couldn't wait to receive calls from Homicide because that usually meant the team would be able to "hit a house" with a warrant.

Warrant service gave the SWAT team a chance to break out the automatic weapons, the battering rams, and the flash/bang grenades. In short, it gave them a chance to do what they did best: locate, subdue, and detain high-risk offenders. Homicide suspects were top on the list.

"Oh gee, John, I don't know," replied Tony. "We'd have to suit up, break out the heavy artillery, and smash some poor taxpayer's door in. We were really looking forward to sitting in the operations room and watching cooking shows."

"Well, if it's too much trouble…"

"Right. Do you have a location for us?"

"Yep. I have the name of the doer, the address, and the name of a relative of the doer who may be in the residence."

"Okay. Fax the stuff over, and we'll scout out the location this afternoon. What time do you want to go in?"

"Six a.m. Early bird catches the toad," replied Bell.

"You got it. I'll give you a call later today to set up the staging area for tomorrow."

"Thanks, Tony. Be safe," Bell said before hanging up.

Officer Tyreek Jackson was not the type of person who easily blended into an environment. Standing just over six-six, Jackson weighed in at a solid 240 pounds, all muscle. The captain of the unit had once said SWAT teams were built specifically with Tyreek in mind. Jackson usually carried the battering ram when the team hit a house, although he could have just as easily functioned as one and smashed through the doors with his lowered shoulder. Tonight, however, he was relegated to scout duty with his partner, Bobby McPhillips. Bobby was shorter than Tyreek but not as muscular. He was more of an athletic type, with a runner's physique, red hair, and such fair skin that Tyreek jokingly referred to him as "the whitest man in America." Whiteness notwithstanding, Bobby could run like a deer, and he usually covered the rear exits in case a suspect tried to beat feet.

The SWAT team almost always did their pre-raid surveillance the night before, usually during the 11:00 p.m. to 7:00 a.m. "last out" shift. The duo received the assignment because they were covering South Philly, and after roll call, they drove their wagon to the target area. Jackson and McPhillips were in full uniform, traveling in their SWAT vehicle, a modified emergency patrol wagon. The officers drove by the house a few times to get a feel for the building, the exits, and the neighborhood in general. The drive-by was the best way to make note of the particulars.

They drew a sketch of the residence and the surrounding area to familiarize the rest of the team, as well as the routes to and from the target house. As a matter of course, they also drew a map of the route from the target to the nearest hospital; that was obviously not the most desirable outcome, but it was always a distinct possibility. Pennsylvania Hospital, the oldest hospital in the nation, was at 8th and Spruce Streets, and it was the closest should anyone need prompt medical attention.

Jackson communicated with Sergeant Capelli via Bluetooth headset, dictating his and Bobby's observations of the location.

"Yeah, Sarge, ya got me?" Tyreek asked.

"I got you, Ty. How close are you to the residence?"

"Bobby and I will be driving by the place in a minute. Passyunk Avenue may be a good staging area. I mean, it's still South Philly, but the intersection shouldn't be a mob scene at 6:00 a.m. - that is, unless your people want to flood the Italian Market at sun up."

Tony agreed. On a good day, parking in South Philadelphia was notoriously bad. On a bad day...well, there wasn't even a reason to bother.

"Yo," Tony replied, "you gotta get there pretty early to get the good *capicola*!"

Tyreek continued, "Okay, we've got a three-story straight-through row home, with a covered porch and bay window out front. There are two front bedroom windows on the second and third floors and a breezeway between the target house and the next house west. There is a wall blocking the breezeway, about six feet tall."

Tony replied, "Okay. Impressions?"

"Bobby thinks the rear team should approach eastbound, against traffic. Duff and Oswald can hop the wall and cover the rear pretty easy if they use the neighbor's front steps. We'll come in westbound and take the front door when we're ready. The porch isn't enclosed, so it's just a matter of getting from the wall to the door, maybe ten feet."

Tony was furiously taking notes and gave a grunt in agreement. He stopped, scratched his nose, and said, "Rear?"

Tyreek replied, "It looks like there's a rear door that opens to a small backyard. No alleyway that I can see, so we can lock it down easily."

"Well, that's good news," Tony said. "John Bell said the doer is kind of a putz, but I'll sleep better knowing we can keep folks penned in. See if you can grab any more intel on the house before heading in. And yes, since it's only midnight, I expect you to stop at Geno's on the way back. I like my cheesesteaks with Cheez Whiz and onions."

"Yes, sir!" Tyreek replied.

The next morning, the staging area on Passyunk Avenue, a short walk from the doer's house, was humming with activity. After the SWAT team suited up, they went over the plan of entry. Because it was a two-story residence, there were eleven team members: three for the first floor, three for the second floor, two in the front, and two in the back. Finally, there was one man known as the "breacher" – Tyreek Jackson, in this case - who would actually take the door.

Bell was pacing back and forth at the staging area. A giant cup of hot black coffee, combined with the usual adrenalin rush that accompanied an impending SWAT operation, served as an effective tonic against the fatigue that accompanies round-the-clock cases such as the Myers one. He kept glancing at his watch. *Where the hell is Nicole?* She'd phoned him early that morning to tell him that her car was acting up and that Jeff would drive her meet him at headquarters, but if she missed them there, she'd see him at the staging area. *If she's any later, she's going to miss the whole thing, and that would be a shame since she's put so much work into it. She deserves to see this toad go down.*

He was distracted from his thoughts about his partner by the arrival of Tony Capelli, flanked by Tyreek Jackson and Bobby McPhillips. The three of them were decked out in typical SWAT black battle dress uniforms (BDUs), complete with Kevlar helmets and combat boots. All the officers were well armed, and they had their game faces painted on; they knew every entry made by the team was dangerous, no matter who was on the other side of the door.

Tony looked around. "Where's your partner?"

"I don't know."

Tony chuckled. "Maybe she's still putting on her makeup."

Bell looked sideways at him through narrowed eyes and said, "She's going to kick your ass for that."

Tony laughed. "Probably, and I'm not sure I can take her." Then he waved his hand expansively toward the house that was their target. "Well, we can't wait around much longer. My guys are in place, and they're chomping at the bit."

Bell looked at his watch again. Tony was right: they couldn't wait on Nicole any longer. She'd be upset at missing out, but time was running short, and they had to get moving if the raid was going to be successful. He nodded. "Okay. Go for it."

Tony nodded. "We'll signal when it's all clear." He handed Bell a police radio tuned to the tactical channel. Accompanied by Tyreek and Bobby, he rounded the corner, his own radio clutched to his mouth.

Bell watched from a distance as the team members lined up at their respective places. The next few minutes crawled by as he waited for the raid to commence. At one time, Bell had considered putting in a transfer to the SWAT team, but he'd realized that just catching the bad guys wasn't enough. He was also motivated by dissecting the criminal mind, especially when it came to murder. *Why do they perpetrate their crimes? What makes one human take the life of another?* Bell devoured true crime books in his spare time, and he had a number of criminal psychology books in his bookcase at home, all of which he read and read again to better understand the darkness that so often penetrates the human soul.

But there was more to it than understanding what makes murderers tick. There was the element of justice for victims and the loved ones they left behind. Bell thought about Leon and Norma Myers. They might not have seen their nephew much in recent years, but they obviously loved him and had been devastated by his death. There would be other relatives and childhood friends who would attend his funeral and ask the eternal question: *"Why? Why our Kevin?"* And the quest for that answer, an answer friends and family members always deserve, was what drove Detective John Bell.

Sometimes he found those answers, and other times he did not, but he would never stop looking.

His reverie was interrupted by the sound of chaos. Bell looked around the corner and saw the breacher, Tyreek Jackson, who had forced the door open with his battering ram, step aside while the other two officers entered the residence. The first officer, Bobby McPhillips, held a Heckler & Koch MP5 submachine gun, while the second carried a city-issued .45-caliber Glock 21 pistol. While he couldn't see them, Bell knew the rear team was carrying Glocks and a shotgun, just in case they faced any opponents of the canine variety. In this instance, M-84 stun grenades, flash/bangs, were not in use because they were only needed in high-risk warrants.

Early risers who were either out for their morning jog or on their way to work gawked as best they could behind the cordon of officers keeping them at bay. Within just a few minutes, the radio in his hand crackled, and Tony's familiar voice came over the airwaves.

"You're clear to come in."

Despite receiving the all-clear, Bell moved forward cautiously, with his gun drawn. He trusted Tony Capelli and his team, but there was always the chance that something could go wrong. As he entered the house on Catharine Street, he saw a terrified Alice Durkin, garbed in a long floral nightdress, surrounded by officers and cowering on the couch. Bell could see a cup of coffee splattered on the carpet in front of her. One of the men jerked his head toward the stairs, and Bell made his way to the second floor into what he assumed to be the Durkins' bedroom.

Inside that room, Reginald Durkin was being held at bay in a corner next to the closet. Clad only in an undershirt and a pair of khaki pants, it was apparent that he'd been caught in the act of getting dressed. When he saw Bell enter the room, he attempted to bluster his way through his fear. "What's going on here? My lawyer is going to hear about this."

"Oh, you have a lawyer? Good." He began the recitation. "Reginald Durkin, I'm placing you under arrest for the murder of Kevin Myers. You have the right to remain silent. Anything you say can and will be used against you in a court of law..."

As Bell finished the Mirandas, Reginald's mouth clamped shut, and his face went pale. He looked around frantically, but upon realizing he wasn't going anywhere on his own power, his shoulders slumped, and he didn't fight when a pair of handcuffs was placed upon his wrists.

As they brought Reginald down the stairs, his wife's eyes widened, and tears began to roll down her cheeks. "Reggie?" she said tentatively. But her husband ignored her as he was pushed out the door and into the waiting patrol wagon.

Less than an hour later, Bell was amidst the ugly green walls of the interview room, sitting across from Reginald and his lawyer. A manila folder reposed on the table in front of him.

Nicole still had not shown up, and she had not called him or anyone else. He was beginning to worry, as it was not like her at all. *Is she ill? Problems at home? She has been acting strangely lately.* As concerned as he was, however, he forced himself to set that worry aside for the moment. He was about to get some answers to his questions about the Myers case – or at least he hoped so.

In Nicole's strange absence, Bell had asked Detective Brian Karpinsky to sit in with him on the interview.

Across the table from the two detectives sat Reginald Durkin and his lawyer, one Robert Gagliano. Clad in a cheap brown suit with a loud tie, he didn't exactly look like the high-roller type, but Bell never went by appearances. Clarence Darrow, one of the most famous defense lawyers of all time, had a somewhat sloppy, homespun look that was at odds with his keen intellect and ability to move juries and judges with his eloquence.

Bell began. "So, Reg, where were you last Friday night?"

Reginald sighed heavily. "We've been through all this. Like I told you, I closed the restaurant at 11 o'clock and was home by 11:30. Didn't you speak to my wife?"

"We did."

"So what's the problem?"

"Problem is, she can't remember when you came home."

"What do you mean? I told you, she was watching television when I arrived."

"Maybe the television was on, but she wasn't watching it. I hate to tell you this, Reg, but your wife is having an affair. She is in love with a tall, dark, and handsome type who goes by the name of 'Mr. Chivas.'"

"What in the hell are you talking about?"

"Reggie, your wife admitted to one of our detectives that she has a bit of a drinking problem and that she was asleep on the couch around 9 o'clock - asleep, passed out, or whatever you wanna call it. Anyway, she said you coached her on what to say to and that she complied because she didn't think you were capable of murder. She didn't want you to get in trouble."

"I'd like to remind you that my client hasn't been convicted of anything yet," the lawyer interjected pompously.

Bell ignored him. "Well, Reg? We're waiting."

Reginald's tongue flicked out, and he licked his lips in a manner that reminded Bell of a lizard. "Well, she does drink a little too much sometimes, and she's kind of a lightweight but that's probably why she's confused about what happened that night."

"Well, in that case, can anyone else verify your whereabouts after you closed the restaurant? Anyone other than your unconscious, coached wife?"

"No."

"Strike two, genius. Actually, someone else can."

"What?" Reginald was clearly startled.

"I said there is someone else can verify your whereabouts after you left the restaurant."

"Huh? Who?"

"Lawrence Jenkins and Daryl Davis. We had an interesting little chat with them yesterday, and let me tell you, they couldn't stop flapping their gums."

Beads of sweat began to form on Reginald's forehead, but he remained silent.

Bell continued. "According to those fine, upstanding young citizens, you ran up to the apartment and asked Kevin to come down to help you move some boxes into the alley behind the kitchen. When he did, Daryl jumped out from behind the dumpster and strangled him with a belt. They fell down during the struggle, which explains the motor oil found on the front of Kevin's shirt."

Reginald's breath was becoming short and shallow, but still he said nothing. Bell continued to recount the tale told to him by Lawrence and Daryl. "Once he was dead, Daryl and Lawrence loaded him into the trunk of a car – a vehicle you'd instructed your loyal employees to steal two weeks earlier - and then they staged the accident on Jasper Street."

"This is all very interesting," Robert Gagliano interjected, "but what's my client's motive? Why on Earth would he murder a young man in his employ?"

"Funny you should ask," Bell said grimly. "It seems Mr. Durkin hatched an interesting scheme to score a large sum of cash in a hurry."

"Why would I do that? My restaurant is doing fine, and-" Reginald was hushed by his lawyer.

"Sure, fine for a man with simple enough tastes, but is it doing well enough for a man with a high-maintenance wife, a home, and a little piece of ass on the side? Do you realize, Mr. Gagliano, that your client has racked up thousands and thousands of dollars on his credit card receiving, uh, specialized attention at Dalia's Delights?"

Judging from his face, it was clear that Robert Gagliano did not.

Bell opened the manila folder and passed a sheet of paper over to the lawyer.

"Take a look. This is a copy of Mr. Durkin's credit card bill."

Gagliano blustered, "Lots of people have overextended credit. This proves nothing."

"On its own, perhaps you're right, but paired with testimony from Lawrence and Daryl that they went to an insurance agency so Daryl could pose as Kevin Myers and take out a $500,000 life insurance policy listing your client as the beneficiary, I'd say it proves quite a bit." He shoved another piece of paper in front of the lawyer, who snatched it up quickly. "And yes, we received this copy from Steve Simmons, the insurance broker. Fortunately for us, he has a good memory for faces. When he saw Kevin's picture in the paper, he realized it wasn't the same man who'd walked into his office claiming to be Kevin Myers just a couple of months ago."

"Say nothing," Gagliano instructed his client, holding up his hand to hush Durkin, who was about to intervene. "And just why would these two men agree to such a scheme?"

"A share in the profits, of course. What else? Strike three, jerk-off."

Reginald lowered his face into his hands as Brian, realizing Bell was finished, signaled the awaiting corrections officers to accompany Reginald to the detention center to be fingerprinted, photographed, and searched thoroughly.

Brian slapped Bell on the back, and Bell smiled crazily. Of course, if Gagliano were as good a lawyer as Clarence Darrow, Reginald Durkin would either be found not guilty or, at the very least, be given a life sentence rather than the death penalty. Nevertheless, Bell could feel the familiar buzz of a closed case starting to set in. While it was a bit early to go out boozing, he definitely would be heading over to The Call Box later, along with Nicole, Brian, Bill, Tony, and anyone else he could dig up for a celebratory drink.

He sighed and turned to Brian. "Well, now comes the paperwork." As the two men made for the door, Officer Roberts from the front desk rushed into the room, clutching a slip of paper. His face was pale, and his light brown hair was in disarray.

"Slow down, Jim," Bell admonished him jokingly. "There'll be plenty of time for congratulations later at The Call Box. Care to join us?"

Jim shook his head. "I have a message for you. It's about Nicole."

Bell's nagging worry about his partner came back in a rush, killing the buzz. "What is it?"

"There's been an…an accident."

"WHAT?"

"An accident. Earlier this morning, she and her husband were crossing the intersection of Grant and the Boulevard when a delivery truck ran a red light."

Bell thought about Jeff Ellis's pride and joy, a red Nissan 350Z, being slammed into by a delivery truck. His stomach lurched. "Why the hell didn't you tell me before?"

"Right before a major arrest?"

He was right, of course, and Bell knew it. They were just following standard practice. "Where are they?"

"They're at Aria Torresdale."

As Bell made to rush out of the room, Jim reached out and grabbed his arm. "John, before you go, you should know…uh, Jeff didn't make it."

"Oh God. And Nicole?" Bell's voice cracked.

"She survived, but she's in critical condition."

Without waiting to hear more, Bell ran out of the interview room as Brian and Jim stared silently at his retreating figure.

Bell crept into the darkened room. The sound of a respirator and other machines clicking and whirring made him feel slightly nauseated. His grandfather had died of cancer when Bell was only ten years old, and he'd spent his final days in the hospital, hooked up to various machines and monitors. Ever since then, Bell was wary of hospitals, despite knowing that not everyone who left one did so with a tag on his toe and covered by a sheet.

Only one bed was occupied, and a chair next to that bed was occupied by a woman. She looked up and saw Bell and rose to greet him.

"John, thank you so much for coming." Nicole's mother hugged him tightly.

As she pulled away, Bell could see that she seemed to have aged ten years since he'd last seen her just a few months prior.

"I'm only sorry I couldn't be here sooner." Bell looked down at the pale, still figure of Nicole on the bed. He forced himself to ask the question. "Is she...is she in a coma?"

"No, thank God," Sally Petrec whispered, wiping the corner of her eye with a crumpled tissue. She was, in looks, an older version her daughter, but her ash-blonde hair had a substantial amount of gray in it and was shorter, cut in a chin-length bob. "She's asleep at the moment. They pumped her full of morphine. She has a concussion and a few cracked ribs."

Bell let his breath out in a giant *whoosh* and ran a hand through his short brown hair. He was relieved; her injuries could have been much more serious. "Does she...did they tell her about Jeff?"

"Not yet." She sniffled. "She was unconscious when she was brought in, and even during the short time she was conscious, it didn't seem like the right time to tell her. I'm still in shock. Jeff was like a son to me, and they were so happy together." Tears were rolling down her cheeks. "How am I going to tell her?"

Bell shook his head, blinking back his own tears. "I don't know," he said quietly. He couldn't take his eyes off of the prone figure in the bed.

"His parents have been notified and they're on their way down from Pittsburgh." She paused. "But that's not all."

Bell wrenched his gaze away from his partner. "There's more? How much worse could it get?"

Sally was struggling to keep her voice from shaking. "The doctor said...oh God, John...She had a miscarriage."

"A...a what?"

"A miscarriage. Nicole was almost two months into her pregnancy."

"Pregnancy? But...but how could she be? I mean-"

"She hadn't told me either, and I don't think Jeff knew. I'm sure he'd have been shouting it from the rooftops. He was so looking forward to being a father, but now..."

Bell grasped her tightly, feeling the dampness of her tears seep through his shirt as she sobbed uncontrollably. As he held Nicole's mother, he thought back to the odd way his partner had been behaving over the past week or so: more tired than usual, a slightly touchy attitude, not imbibing with her colleagues at The Call Box, and the occasional far-away look. No one thing pointed to anything in particular, but it all made sense in retrospect.

Nicole was pregnant, planning to be a mother. She'd be a damn good one too. But now? God. Not only is her husband dead, but her baby is gone as well. Why? What the hell is wrong with this world when one stupid moment, a momentary distraction on the part of some idiot truck driver, can end two lives and endanger another? Meanwhile, far too many heartless bastards like Drew Nichols roam the streets, doing drugs, raising hell, and beating the life out of defenseless old women. And what about losers like Reginald Durkin, preying upon people like Kevin Myers, taking advantage of their good nature and gullibility? Bell thought it was disgusting.

"It's not fair," he muttered.

Sally's weeping had subsided. She looked up at him. "I know, John, but I'm sure your parents warned you about that when you were growing up. Too many times, life just isn't fair. That's just the way it is."

Bell sighed. "I know, but it still sucks."

Chapter Thirteen

As Bell entered the hospital room, clad in a blue polo shirt and jeans and bearing a bouquet of flowers, Nicole was in her bed and staring at a mindless game show that was playing on the television. He added his yellow roses to her growing collection of arrangements on the windowsill and sat down in the chair next to her bed. She continued to watch as Drew Carey said, "Come on down!" for the millionth time and another screaming contestant made her way down the aisle for her chance to win on *The Price is Right*.

Bell watched her for a few moments, unsure how to break the ominous silence. Hospital lighting wasn't flattering at the best of times, but it wouldn't have mattered if she'd been outside in a meadow under the full sunlight. Her blonde hair was lank, her face was drained of color, and her eyes – her striking blue eyes – seemed devoid of life. Blood seeped through a bandage on the left side of her forehead. As he racked his brains trying to come up with a way to start a conversation, Nicole spoke abruptly, although her eyes remained glued to the television set.

"I wasn't sure I wanted it anyway."

For a moment, Bell didn't know what she was talking about. When it dawned on him, he was stunned into silence, but that didn't seem to matter to Nicole, who was watching an overweight brunette named Shannon play Lucky Seven in an attempt to win a car. *Wait…was she considering…abortion?* Perhaps she saw the concern on his face out of the corner of her eye because she continued, "And no, that's not what I mean."

"I wouldn't have done that. It's just…it's just that…well, even though we wanted children, it wasn't planned, and I wasn't prepared to deal with it. I suppose…" Her eyes took on the same far-away look he'd noticed once or twice during their investigation, before he had known of the pregnancy. "I suppose…" she continued, "I guess I would have gotten used to the idea and it would have been okay. Jeff would have been thrilled. He talked about having children and being a father. Of course, none of that matters now, does it?" she finished in a flat voice.

Not having grown up in a particularly close family, Bell was at a loss as to what to do or say, which bothered him because he was probably closer to Nicole than to anyone else in his life, including his parents. Normally he and she could talk about almost anything, but nothing of this magnitude had touched their relationship before. His breakup with Renee was absolutely nothing by comparison, and they had talked about that nonstop for weeks as he healed from the heartbreak and shame of it. Nicole had been there for him, and now he feared he would be unable to be there for her in the same way. Perhaps if she had started crying, it would have given him an opening to hug her and whisper some appropriate responses, but her unfamiliar, distant manner was not conducive to such closeness, so he remained in his chair, hands clasped tightly in his lap.

Screaming and applause from the television diverted his attention for a moment. Shannon had won her car. As he watched her jump up and down and hug the host, he heard Nicole speak again.

"Will you be at the funeral?"

"Of course." Bell paused. "I've been keeping in touch with your mom. She told me you're being released tomorrow and that the service is being planned for Saturday. I'll be there, and so will Bill, Brian, Jim, and some of the others. Sergeant Baker will be there too."

"Thanks."

A commercial for laundry detergent flashed on the screen, with a perky housewife extolling the virtues of whiter than white socks. Nicole spoke again with unusual brusqueness. "What happened?"

"Huh?"

"The case? Durkin?"

"Oh, that scumbag." Bell related the tale of the SWAT raid on the Durkins' house on Catharine Street, how Durkin had ignored his wife when he was taken out in handcuffs, and how, when confronted with the evidence of his crime, he had simply sat there in his undershirt with his face in his hands, his shoulders slumped in defeat.

"We have the testimony of those two losers who were in on it with him, as well as the testimony of the insurance agent. It's a solid case. I'm pretty sure we'll nail him in court."

"What about Kevin's aunt and uncle?"

"They're happy that we made an arrest." Bell thought back to his meeting with Leon and Norma Myers the day before. Norma had been apologetic about their behavior the day they had been at the police station and the activist group Blaq Unity had seemed to turn them against the police. Leon had looked as though he might be a bit regretful, too, but he wouldn't say so, allowing his tearful wife to say what needed to be said. Perhaps it was pride, Bell thought, or perhaps he really did feel that the police generally give blacks the shaft. Unfortunately, Bell had no control over that attitude. He knew he gave each and every case the attention it deserved, regardless of the victim's or defendant's race or creed. That was all he could do.

"The morgue is releasing the body, and it's being sent down to Georgia. The Myers couple is scheduled to fly back down there this morning."

They sat in silence for a few more minutes, neither one knowing how to breach the unexpected gulf that had sprung up between them.

A nurse entered, wearing white pants and a brightly patterned top. The cheeriness of her outfit somehow seemed out of place. "I'm here to change your dressings," she said briskly.

Bell took that as his cue to leave and rose from his chair. On impulse, he bent down and dropped a quick kiss on Nicole's cheek.

She started slightly and broke her gaze away from the television and looked straight at him.

His heart ached with the knowledge that there was nothing he could do about the sadness he saw there.

"See you soon," he murmured, and in a few quick steps he was out of the room.

Nicole endured the nurse's ministrations silently. After the woman had changed the bandages and checked Nicole's vital signs, she left Nicole alone with yet another game show. She grabbed the remote and turned the television off, unable to ward off her thoughts any longer.

The seemingly endless parade of well-wishers, friends, and family members had drained her of whatever inner strength she had, and Nicole was thankful to be by herself for a little while, though she knew her mother would be by again in the afternoon.

She thought back to when she'd awakened from her collision and drug-induced slumber, confused momentarily as to why she was lying in a hospital bed with needles and tubes sticking out of her and a respirator tube up her nose. Seeing her mother huddled in the chair nearby had brought everything back in a rush. Her car hadn't started the morning of the planned SWAT raid, so she'd asked Jeff for a ride to headquarters.

They hadn't talked much, both being a bit sleepy, and anyhow, neither one of them were ever particularly chatty in the mornings. Jeff had stopped at a red light at the corner of Grant Avenue and Roosevelt Boulevard, and moments later, when the light turned green and Jeff accelerated, there was a flash of horror when an Acme grocery store delivery truck barreled into them. After that, she could recall nothing other than waking up at the hospital.

Nicole couldn't remember having ever felt so numb and empty. When her father had died, she recalled the sadness and grief that had threatened to engulf her and her entire family. Despite her youth, however, she'd been able to deal with it because of her need to be strong and supportive for her mother and brother. But there was no one who needed her support now. Jeff, the love of her life, was gone, and so was the baby they should have had together.

The thought of the baby made her sit up, and she winced at the stab of pain in her abdomen and the twinge of guilt that plagued her conscience. *Could it really be that less than a week ago that I was unsure of wanting the living being that had been growing inside me – a life that's no longer there, snuffed out by a damn delivery driver?*

Had she had time to get used to the idea, Nicole likely would have become excited at the prospect of becoming a mother. Nevertheless, because of her initial inner turmoil upon hearing the news from her gynecologist, Nicole hadn't yet told anyone of her pregnancy. The haunted look in her mother's eyes when she stood by as the doctor told Nicole that she'd lost the baby made the loss of Jeff nearly unbearable, because now there would be nothing of him left for her to love and cherish.

Jeff! she cried inwardly. Jeff had died unaware that he would have been a father. *Was I too selfish not telling him? Oh my God! I had deprived him of the pleasure of pending fatherhood. He would have been so happy to know. He should have known! I should have told him while he was still alive!* She decided that she should be dead, too, seeing as she was as good as dead inside.

The survivor's guilt she felt was compounded by the knowledge that she felt cut off from Bell, who was not only her partner, but one of her closest friends. She had girlfriends, of course, some of whom had been by to visit as well, but plumbing the dumpster of human behavior without developing a tight bond with the person who was dumpster diving right alongside was nearly impossible.

Even still, she'd been unable to respond to Bell's mute attempts to connect. He'd tried to look her in the eye – something her girlfriends had all distinctly avoided – yet she'd stared right past him, as though he was a stranger on the street.

Thinking back to that afternoon at The Call Box, Nicole recalled thinking about how attractive Bell was and wondering what he would be like as a father. Her stomach suddenly felt sour, as though she'd been at the carnival and gone on the Tilt-a-Whirl right after eating a chili dog and cotton candy. Her husband wasn't even in the ground yet, and there she was, imagining what another man would be like as a father.

Nicole's dry eyes wandered over to the windowsill, where brightly colored bouquets with little cards stuck in plastic holders brought false cheer to the sterile room. Her gaze fell upon the dozen yellow roses that Bell had brought. *My favorite. He remembered my favorite.* And with that thought, she burst into uncontrollable sobs.

A day later, Bell sat at his desk, swirling cold coffee around in a Styrofoam cup and staring at the Kevin Myers file in front of him. Nicole had been released from the hospital and had gone to stay with her mother while she continued to recuperate from her injuries. She was on sick leave, of course, which would be followed up by bereavement leave. He'd see her at the funeral, but he didn't expect to see much of her until she returned to work in several weeks.

Opening the file, he flipped listlessly through the papers inside until a photocopy of the picture of Kevin in his Army uniform caught his eye. He stopped and stared at it. *Poor kid. He lost his parents in a freak accident while he was off fighting for his country. Then he comes back home to find that his friends aren't really his friends, and he can't find a better job than working as some drudge in a crummy greasy spoon, for a man who took advantage of his easygoing, gullible nature – a slime ball who had him killed so he could collect enough insurance money to pay off his debts at a strip club – and then some.*

What a waste.

Bell swallowed the last of the coffee and crumpled the cup, tossing it into a nearby garbage can. He normally would have felt elated at the successful outcome to a case, but Nicole's plight was naturally a killjoy. He decided that perhaps he'd give her a call a couple of days after the funeral, just to see how she was doing. *Perhaps I'll–*

His cell phone went off, interrupting his thoughts. Bringing it up to his ear, he clicked the green button. "John Bell."

"John, it's Billy Flynn. I have a couple news items you might find interesting."

"Shoot."

"First, Drew Nichols got into a fight in jail. Apparently, some of his neighbors behind bars don't appreciate his white supremacist views. Had the crap beaten out of him. He's in intensive care."

Bell sighed. It was hard to feel sympathetic for someone like Drew Nichols. Sure, he'd had his fair share of hard luck, but a lot of people grew up in similar circumstances and didn't end up as antisocial losers who took their anger out on the rest of the world at large. "Tough break," he said noncommittally. "I hope somebody tried to give him CPR in his ear. What else?"

"Reginald Durkin's dead."

"What? How?"

"Hung himself in his cell with a sheet. They found him first thing this morning."

It was a good thing Bell had finished his coffee; otherwise, it would have come spewing out of his mouth. "Wow," was all Bell could come up with. "Thanks for letting me know."

"How's Nicole doing?" Billy asked.

Bell could hear the rumble of traffic over the phone.

"As well as can be expected. I saw her yesterday."

"Jeff was one of the good guys. I'm going to try to make it on Saturday, but if I don't, give her my best, will you?"

"Of course." The two men exchanged goodbyes, and then Bell hung up. *So Reginald took the coward's way out, denying Kevin Myers's family the satisfaction of their day in court. Shit. Well, at least he saved the taxpayers of Pennsylvania some of their hard-earned cash.*

Chapter Fourteen

John Bell sat at his desk, staring at his computer screen. The Myers Investigation Report 75-49 was open but he was not in the mood to type at the moment. His mind was wandering; he didn't know how long it had been out on tour, but he did realize he was feeling rather distant. Besides, he had thirty days to finish the report, so there was no rush.

Sergeant Baker came up and tapped him on the shoulder, snapping Bell out of his trance.

"That 49 isn't going to write itself, you know," Baker said.

"No, it isn't, sir." Bell deadpanned.

"Well, are you going to get started or what? The captain wants these reports submitted in a timely fashion."

"Sarge," Bell replied, "we just closed the Myers case today. We helped close the Nichols case too. And now, my partner is lying in a hospital bed, mourning the death of her husband and the loss of her unborn child. I think the captain will understand if I don't finish a damned 49 for a couple of fucking days."

Baker, realizing he'd crossed a line, looked down at his shoes.

"Look, John, why don't you take off for the day, clear your head? Go see Nicole," he said, "and give her my best."

"Thanks, Sergeant. I'll see you tomorrow."

Bell gathered his things, put on his coat, and dejectedly walked out of Police Headquarters. The satisfaction of the clearance was not enough to overcome the grief he was feeling for Nicole. He was walking toward his car with his eyes down when he almost ran into Jamal Taylor of Blaq Unity. Bell looked up, said, "Excuse me," and made a move to sidestep Taylor.

Taylor, however, insisted on blocking his way.

"I want to talk to you about the Myers case," Taylor began.

"I'm not in the mood," Bell snapped. "Go talk to Sergeant Baker. I'm off the clock."

"Fine," replied Taylor, "but I want you to know we're not going away until that piece of white trash is tried and convicted for Kevin's murder."

Bell was too tired to argue, but he couldn't pass up another opportunity to poke the voice of Blaq Unity.

"Well, there's not going to be a trial."

"What?" Taylor screamed. "Are you telling me he got a plea deal? A man is dead – a black man, yes, but a man nonetheless – and somebody pleas their way out of it? What kind of justice system is it when-"

"No," Bell replied. "There isn't going to be a trial because Reginald Durkin is dead. He hung himself inside his cell. Now get away from me before I lock you up."

"Lock me up? For what?"

"Disorderly conduct."

Taylor opened his mouth to argue, but he thought better of it. Instead, he watched John Bell walk to his car, get in, and drive away.

His cell phone rang again. Thinking it might be Billy again with something he'd forgotten to share, Bell answered it quickly. "John Bell."

"John?" a female voice queried.

Bell felt his stomach tighten up. *No*, he said to himself. *Of all days, please, not today.* It took everything in him to resist the temptation to hang up. "Yes?"

"John, it's me, Renee. Can we talk?"

Bell closed his eyes and sighed deeply. "I guess."

About the Authors:

Pam Meister graduated from Western Connecticut State University with a degree in communications. An online political and social commentator since 2005, she has also been a lover of the true crime and crime novel genres for over a decade. She lives in Connecticut with her family.

Shawn Goodwin has been a member of the Philadelphia Police Department since 1994. He is a graduate of Saint Joseph's University, and during his college career, he proudly served as a writer, features editor, and editor-in-chief of the university newspaper, *The Hawk*. He was the official satirist at Family Security Matters for nearly three years and has been blogging since 1995. Shawn lives in Philadelphia with his wife and four children.

Made in the USA
Charleston, SC
10 July 2012